THESE DEMENTED LANDS

Alan Warner was born in Oban and brought up there. His first book, *Morvern Callar*, was a critical triumph and won a Somerset Maugham Award; the novel has now been filmed by the BBC. He currently lives in Co. Wicklow and is working on a third novel.

BY ALAN WARNER

Morvern Callar
These Demented Lands

Alan Warner

THESE DEMENTED LANDS

VINTAGE

ACKNOWLEDGEMENTS

*Thanks to the Scottish Arts Council for a bursary
and the K. Blundell Trust for an Authors' Foundation Award*

Published by Vintage 1998

2 4 6 8 10 9 7 5 3 1

First published in Great Britain by
Jonathan Cape Ltd, 1997

Vintage
Random House, 20 Vauxhall Bridge Road,
London SW1V 2SA

Random House Australia (Pty) Limited
20 Alfred Street, Milsons Point, Sydney
New South Wales 2061, Australia

Random House New Zealand Limited
18 Poland Road, Glenfield,
Auckland 10, New Zealand

Random House South Africa (Pty) Limited
Endulini, 5A Jubilee Road, Parktown 2193, South Africa

Random House UK Limited Reg. No. 954009

A CIP catalogue record for this book
is available from the British Library

ISBN 0 09 957791 7

Printed and bound in Great Britain by
Cox & Wyman, Reading, Berkshire

For Mark Richard,
Michael Ondaatje . . . thanks.
Juan Carlos Onetti (1909–94)

'Multitudes of people! Walking up the hills!'
  In the Name of the Father, Black Grape

'We went down into the waste, and accordingly began to make our toilsome and devious travel towards the eastern verge.'
  Kidnapped, R. L. Stevenson

FIRST TEXT
Part One

First Night

I got near the island; Ferryman was about to ask me to see a ticket when the boat started to sink: 'If it's the return tickets yous have got, best swim for it,' Ferryman bawled then he jamp over the side into blackwater.

It was neardark. Since Ferryman'd cut the outboard engine all was silent; could hear the loose, metal lampshade on the single bulb above the Boat Chandlers at Ferry Slipway. The lampshade was clattering in any gusts before they reached.

A low roll of cloud had circled the island and seemed to hold the luminous dayness in its depths and bulges. You could see the braes: the bare rowans, the dark spruces, larches below the cloud then the true mountainheads above, behind the five silhouettes of the passengers facing me who tilted gently to one side. Water breached the gunwhale and busily began filling the bottom of the boat.

The blonde kiddy with the sticking plaster over her eye who'd been staring at me since Mainland (apart from suddenly turning to spew then spit over the side); the telly-aerial repairers who'd been so mortal and rackety; the fat man with the cigar and huge metal-looking crucifix:

All went straight into silentness.

Big fat man shot up, 'Car ferry's wake's gone and sunk us.' He hauled his crucifix and chain above the baldiness then tossed them over the side; the tip of his cigar glowed brighter as he rose up by the oarlocks, rocked the boat then stepped overboard. I turned away from his splash and saw the huge black ship vanishing into the dark Upsound, could still read the words on the stern:

PSALM 23
Greenock

I looked down and saw the ghostly-pale glow of the petrol tank – no more than a plastic jerry-can – that in eight months' time I would be reminded of by a catheter bag (the drop petrol in the bottom like thick, lazy urine).

I savvied right enough that the petrol tank would keep me afloat so, with the telly-aerial repairers sat like daft apeths, I stepped forward and drew a real squeal from the blonde child as I bunched her ribbons and ponytails in both my hands and hauled her up to chest level, threw a left arm round; she kneed me on the left bosom as I swung, huffed out a puff and grabbed the petrol-tank handle with the right hand – in two steps we were up
on the transom, leaping, then,
for the split second,
soaring
over moonless nightwater,
with the blonde hair of the child in my arms,

4

the brightest thing in such
darknesses.

When you first hit freezing darkwater there's a strangeness
and instant when you feel and see nothing, then that liquidy
seep in through the most porous bits: top of jeans, front of
whatevertop, slowly, slowly down your back under the air
bubble of your jackets (jacket's . . . jackets': do you need
these comma things??) jacket's shoulders . . . it's certain you
do feel the pull of that new *dread*weight your clothes are
starting to become.

When my wrecked boots hit water I was smiling and the
surface shocked into my face. I'd misjudged the strength of
that long-orangey-rubber-tube-thing connecting the petrol
tank to the outboard and it really breenged us round twisting
my arm behind my back. I shivered, opened eyes: the splash
had turned the little blonde girl's (girls?) hair jet-black. I tried
to yank the jerry-can; the sinking boat tugged back at me
then the cap popped off freeing the petrol tank. I let go the
handle to try turn myself; I just let go for a jiffy, but, with a
sure movement, together, the half-blind child in my arms and
I sank beneath the nightwater.

I opened my eyes in the static and rumble. A landscape of
colours was glissanding on the lunar seabeds way below; my
black legs slowly kicking so thin in silhouette. I hugged that
wee girl tighter to me. A constellation of pinkish bubbles rose
up under my feet then drifted, swole, each bubble's angle
reflecting a diamond nova from both its north and south pole.

In the furthest distances of this universe the rising planets and blue stars from seabed geysers, a huge surface of tiny bubbles, wobbled under us lit by deepest flarings below: a coral reef gone insane in the colours of these killing seas.

Just then Ferryman's boat sank – away there – past us, its bow pointed deaddown and you saw the gilt, hand-painted lettering on its stern flashing a last time in the wildlights before

IN GOD WE TRUST

the black hull darted into a bank of turquoisey bubbles, the orangey fuel pipe, trailing behind – straight up as a plumb line.

Though it forced us deep towards those seabed burnings, I tried to heave-ho the little girl up: shove her surfacewards. I was sorry for our death ... I'd heard around that the drowning could be no so bad but there was that book that had scared me: the *Pincher Martin* book; the book of drowning. Just when I was getting the All Dramatic I felt a trickle of cold on my wrist in naked air, rolled and was on the surface. Bruised-blue sky above was now dark though I was fairly positive there was still a little light when we'd gone under; now was nightimeness so I brought the kiddy onto my chest. The fuel tank was just bob-bobbing beside, I grabbed at it and then the bright and coloured water around us just flickered and switched off like swimming-pool lights.

'What was it?' she whimpered.

I goes, 'I don't know, darling.'

The sticky-on patch had come away in the salt water and a dead eye, like a green jewel of frozen phlegm on some winter pavement, stared down at me from her beautiful little button face.

By holding the handle of the jerry-can to my side and kick-kicking, we curved a shaky course in towards the lonesome single bulb above the door of the Boat Chandlers at Ferry Slipway.

Ahead, a minute point of tangerine light flourished then dulled; through the perishing cold I creaked a nervous smile. Big fat man was grimly wheezing shorewards, the cigar still miraculously alight in his mouth.

'Ahoy there,' I says.

He spoke out the side of his mouth, 'Saint Moluag challenged Saint Columba to a race, from Mainland to this island: first one to touch the land. So they spun across in their coracles and Saint Columba was holding a good lead close to this shore; Saint Moluag took up his axe, chopped off his little finger, hurled it onto the island shouting, "There, *I* touched the shore first."'

He clached out a snigger then sucked on his cigar. I thumped the petrol tank over to him, 'Kick in on this and we'll race you.'

'Race him, race him!' the wee girl was bouncing, flooding water over my bosom. Big fat man took the cigar stub out his mouth and dropped it into the spout of the jerry-can. A ten-foot spew of flame jamp out the cap-hole propelling the fat man furiously towards the shore. He screamed, the orange fountain of light – for a second – lit up other heads, clutching seat-cushions or other stuff, kicking in shorewards to Ferry Slipway.

A patch of burny water sailed away west, upsound, before withering into a shape at the back of my mind. Then I saw it: an echo of the flames up there above the cloud – the ancient and dour light of campfire, high on the ben sides.

Dripping sodden-wet, still holding the child, I booted in the door of the Boat Chandlers and one of the telly-aerial repairers lunged towards me holding out a bottle of Bunnahabhain. I shook head no and let the child down to the ground, 'Lights. I saw such strange lights out there, deep in the waters,' I says.

'The Phosphorous Beds,' the Harbour whispered behind and sort of nodded to the kid at my leg. 'They dumped hundreds of tons of phosphorus bombs in the Sound after the war; last few years they started burning up. Who knows what else's down there. Those colours: divers won't go near; the canisters sometimes come up in lobster pots on fire . . . you see a streamer of white smoke whipping above a well-decker.' The Harbour turned away, spoke even quieter, 'Sometimes, burning phosphorus canisters wash up on the beach, and *sometimes* kiddies find them, you know?'

I nodded. 'Did all get safely ashore?'

'No sign of the Devil's Advocate, Ferryman's way out in the dinghy and we've phoned for Nam the Dam to do a fly-by in his chopper.' The Harbour accepted the whisky bottle offof the redhead telly-aerial repairer.

'Be as well with yon Argonaut and his line,' the redhead says.

The tall one from amongst the telly-aerial repairers squinted at the redhead who explains, 'Argonaut's some kind of crazy salvage-diver-cum-Armada-treasure-hunter from across the island.'

The Harbour says, 'He's a body-finder too; anyone drowns in these waters it's aye Argonaut who can find where the bag of bones'll wash up or where the currents'll have it lying in fathoms.'

The redhead goes, 'Sails round the islands in a kayak with all these words from the bible writ all over.'

'He moves between the islands. Big ships have sighted him in his kayak miles out to sea,' The Harbour tilted back the bottle so its base near touched the ceiling.

The tally one asked, 'Who is that fat guy, some sort of a lawyer or a religious freak, or what?'

The Harbour goes, 'Nah, nah he's a pape from the church. He's the Devil's Advocate: decides who should get to become a saint and who shouldnty and all yon; wandering hills with his tent, researching into saints; canonisation it's called, trying to find out dirt in the past of already-saints . . . he's sort of an investigative journalist for God.'

'Well if he's on the ocean bed getting his eyes ett out by crabs, the church'll be down on this ferry like a shot . . .'

'Shush!' I snapped at the Tall, jerking my head down at the child.

'Is big fat man drowned or all burned up?' the kiddy says.

'That Argonaut,' the Harbour smirked, 'He's pulverised

out the mind on the drugs. He goes down diving on acid, to fix a line on those bodies he finds, and conducts a wee religious service with a flare.'

I kneeled and picked up the wet child, 'Nah, honey, I reckon he's safe and sound and we'll be seeing more of him.'

'Theres gey-few saints to be found on this ruck of an island,' the Harbour grumbled.

'I've got to get her out these clothes.'

'We've no kiddies' gear. Wrap her in a towel and I'll get those on the heater. As for you, help yourself to the clothes; the most expensive yacht jacket's there, so take one; there's a wee lifejacket in that you can blow up! Italian. As per usual I just bill the ferry company . . .'

'How do you mean, as per usual?'

'Hell, girl, third time this winter the wee boat's been sunk. El Capitain on the *Psalm 23* thinks he's still in the cod war; hasn't left the bridge for months, gets a bottle of malt sent up every morning.'

The quiet one of telly-aerial repairers piped up, 'We were sunk time before, so we took out good luggage insurance this time.'

'Here on the razzle though,' goes Redhead, 'Trek straight up to the Aerial Bothy, check the box and it's the usual fuse blown; phone home to base and tell the suckers it's a major job of about four days; book The Outer Rim Hotel and drink ourselves into the Olympics; claim the booze as expenses then go back up on our last day and fix the fuses . . .'

'Works every time,' says the Tall.

'Mummy and Daddy send the Kongo Express for me at night,' the wee thing smiled. I took her behind the row of waterproofs out the gaze of the drunk telly-aerial repairers though she was so young.

'Aye, pet,' I goes, then, 'Arms to the high sky.' I tugged her top up, the wetness in the lycra squeezing out at her tiny wrists before the sleeves both pop, popped up and dangled. I squeezed the top out. When she bended over: the amazing smooth, perfectcrack of her child-bum. I scoufuled up her ribbons and ponytails with the towel.

After I'd chosen, I took the little girl up back of the Chandlers where there was a mirror. I couldn't even hear the telly-aerial repairers bawling back there. I took off my old, tatty steerhide jacket: all tears and fatherings; I ever-so-gingerly plucked out the CD Walkman. I opened the lid; the girl giggled as water poured out. It was utterly jiggered, and I just took the CD that was Verve: All In The Mind (HUTCD 12), though it was track three, Man Called Sun that I always listened to, if you must know. I slipped it in the pocket with an eye to the future then dropped the Walkman on the floor; she asked if she could have it; I explained it was kaput and all that. My other Verve CDs had been in the carrier bag (lying on the Sound floor, shiny-side-up, reflecting the searing phosphorus colours lifting above them).

I stripped, looked, run my palms down over tum, glanced at the sproglet, but she was fascinated with the buttons on the Walkman; I turned to study the dying suntan, the unshaved legs with a swirl of wet hairs on the backs of thighs. I started looking through what I'd chosen to fully enjoy the . . . the feeling . . . what I would call, in the other words, *La me da igual*, but no, those are the other languages from . . . Down There and the things that happened to me, walking in moonlight with dark sunglasses among forest fires and shooting stars. So in this language I've made this daft deal to tell my story in . . . *La me da igual* . . . how can I say it in the old words? The Indifferent Feeling; yes! The Indifferent Feeling. That's what I had enjoyed as the Harbour let me choose the clothes in the Chandlers. I'd just crammed things in the kitbag he'd given me. The Harbour noted the items down and kept a receipt for himself.

I'd says, 'I'd do anything for some real girl clothes,' but I was stuffing the gear away like it was nobody's business and that's The Indifferent Feeling: heavy men's work-shirts still smelling of their cheap dyes; big baggy-pant boxer shorts, even S too big for me; socks all colours, enough to pad the small good boots I grabbed; and always not caring what colour combinations I was getting, cause The Indifferent Feeling . . . what I call privately *La me da igual*.

You see The Indifferent Feeling mostly in eating places and clothes shops. It's harboured in middle-aged guys who live not pretending anymore. They come in, a wee-bit-overweight guy, grey hairs here and there, money in the pockets but no concessions to fashion – in other words to women. He needs a new jacket so he finds one that fits, throws it on the counter by the till. The assistant tells him the jacket comes in three other colours; the man shrugs, no doubt by now counting out the notes and not even looking at the assistant girl who is young, dead pretty and, as you look at her clothes, carefully dressed – cause that still has meaning. She's got lies she can still believe in, but our friend, well that shrug shows it all. It's not just that I feel free when I live The Indifferent Feeling myself, it's that I find it so attractive in others. When I was way Down There, in those days when I only ate in restaurants, I would see men, those same men who had lived, I would see the indifference they really tried to hide, terrified Life was going sour on them; their smugness was losing its novelty; they stared at a menu that five years before would have given them a pleasing feel. But they had come to understand how childish it was, how little it mattered if they placed A or B inside their mouths and masticated it to a tight bolus. They never ate desserts cause their fragile pride wouldn't allow them to speak out those silly names.

While I'm on about it may as well mention what, to myself, I call The Correspondence Feeling. There's the others I could explain: The Toffee Feeling, The Thin Hair Feeling, The Rudder Feeling, The Cheese Sandwich in the Back of the Car Feeling, The October Afternoon Feeling, Peeling the Tangie Feeling: all the ones that make me me. Aye, The Correspondence Feeling: I had it when we were out there swimming in the Sound and the Devil's Advocate had set fire to the petrol tank . . . no, it started even before that, when my eye lighted on the orange-end glow of his cigar, *then* there was the petrol burning then the light of the campfire up the mountains: 'flame, flame, flame'. Sometimes you see it on a city street: three strangers moving in different directions come adjacent, each has a yellow jacket on so you get this row yellow, then your eye follows along and a huge yellow juggernaut is passing beside so, when the light catches it, *all* is shimmery yellow on the pavement and reflected in the shop windows . . .

When I materialised front-of-shop and declared, 'I'm looking for The Drome Hotel, that one with the graveyard beside,' The Harbour coughed and the telly-aerial repairers stared at me. I took the dried clothes to dress the girl and when we returned The Harbour cleared his throat again and goes, 'Yonder is Brotherhood's domain.'

'Brotherhood. Brotherhood?' I says the name.

'That's a right weird place out yon, we'd never dream of holing up in it.'

There was a good bit silentness.

The Tall went, 'Who's Brotherhood?'

'He arrived back here piloting on old PBY flying boat; all these French hippy chicks were on board; anchored offof The Outer Rim Hotel, the girls sunbathing up on the wings, diving off then swimming in for lemonades . . .'

'The Sanctions Buster we called him back then, account of his carry-ons down in Africa there; his Dad kept good health and was running The Drome as a decent . . .'

The Harbour laughed and goes, 'Brotherhood's forgotten dream. Young men's dreams that pepper out: of setting up an island casino at The Drome with *Folies Bergère* girls; punters choppered in.' The Harbour snorted, shook his head in sort of despair, 'What he's got is as close as he can get to the pimp he wants to be.'

The Tall and me looked at the Harbour in sort of appeal. I goes, 'What're you meaning?'

'You'll be seeing . . . soon enough, soon enough.'

We stepped outside under the rattling lampshade. The Harbour says, 'You wonnie be needing your kitbag less you plan leaving us, and if that Devil's Advocate doesn't show soon we'll be needing all heads we can get along the shores.'

I went, 'Far is it to The Drome?'

'Don't think about it, lassie. Fifteen mile as crow flies. Over The Interior. Twenty-five round the coast road. On a Saturday night, now, you could get The Disco Bus that circles, gathering all the young ones for their dancing at The Outer Rim. It's a hell of a sight, yon, on the way back, but none's brave enough to get aboard; even High-Pheer-Eeon who swims over from Mainland on his hunting and scavenging missions was found locked in the boot at the garage one Monday morning: Turns out he'd been using the boots to move round the island for weeks, too feart to go upstairs.'

I began to cross the Slip with the little girl's hand in mine. 'Now how do you get home?' I goes.

'You ring the little lectric bell for The Kongo Express.'

'Nah, seriously honey.'

Then we came to the top of the slipway:

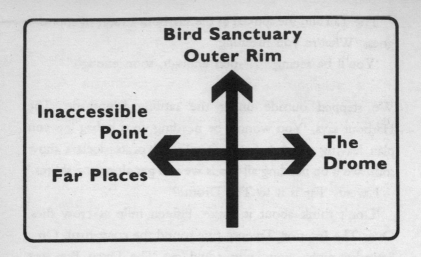

Bird Sanctuary
Outer Rim

Inaccessible
Point

Far Places

The
Drome

It was only months later I'd read His pages, typed on the toy Fisher-Price typewriter, pages dated Wednesday seventeenth, Thursday twenty-second and Friday twenty-third. *His* . . . pages, the one they called the Aircrash Investigator, or the Failed Screenwriter, or the Man From The Department of Transport, even a name: Walnut or Warmer, though one night in The Heated Rooms when I pressed him he says his name was Houlihan. I read in his pages that never had the months, just the useless, mixed-up dates, how he came ashore as a Foot Passenger from the big Weekend-Only car ferry, and of course his eye saw the dent in the bottom right-hand corner of the road sign, where a provisions truck coming off the Slip must have clipped it one.

WEDNESDAY 17TH

if that was his concept of the devil it certainly wasnt mine. My eye lighted on the bashed road sign back at the landing jetty. In its lower right corner it had taken an impact so I stood on tiptoe to squint. It was a forward impact of about ten miles per hour, traces of a green, metal-based paint remained embedded in the reflective coating at the edges of the laceration where the impact had not chipped the insect-eye reflective coating. By examining the crease-lines on the rear of the sign I could tell the impact had been less of a factor than the weight of the vehicle behind it . . . a faster impact would have left less stress-bearing marks in the tensile areas, however the proximity of the edge had allowed the forward impact forces to bleed off the sign. Had impact occurred closer to the centre of the sign, which is free-standing, fixed to two hollow aluminium poles embedded in sea-decayed concrete, the entire sign could have collapsed. By the sudden rightward movement of the impact scar I could tell the vehicle had shifted to the right. By calculating graze depth and presuming aluminium contact without the aid of lab tests (by which I calculated the forward impact speed) I estimate an impact speed of 9.463 m.p.h. and a contact time of 3.768 seconds though it would be difficult to take these results seriously without more time at the site but I'd the disco bus to catch. My calculations are shown on the 22nd and the 23rd. I noticed a 45-gallon drum with an interesting smash in the side but I couldnt be bothered.

I like that sentence: *where a provisions truck coming off the Slip must have clipped it one.*

Beyond the sign, the little girl tugged me to the left and we passed a HISTORIC CASTLE symbol road sign, down a path we came to a railway station but, the weird thing was, it was a miniature station I saw emerging out the dark as the girl pressed the buzzer. The roof of the station only came to my chin and I could see the close-togetherness of the little rails of the track and out the dark wind that moved the looming spruce trees at their tops, came a miniature train with KONGO EXPRESS writ on a brass plate at the front.

'Aye-aye. Wanting dropped anywhere?' The driver looked at me. 'Niagara Falls, Mount Kilimanjaro, Makarikari Salt Pans?' he yelled out a laugh.

'The boat sunk,' I says.

'Watch out for snakes and tigers,' he shrieked, then he shrugged like as if to say sorry, 'It all reminds her ladyship of the good times, when she was beautiful.'

'Can I sleep in the princess's tower?' the girl, who had sat in the little coach behind the driver, covered his eyes with her hands.

'Do you know of the man Brotherhood?'

The driver says, 'John Brotherhood, the Sanctions Buster. He sailed in a rusty old minesweeper – that's how he got started; he was innocent then, and of the crew only Brotherhood and the Captain didn't get seasick. They drank two bottles of rum a day. When they approached those white beaches, Brotherhood stepped out of the bridge; mosquitoes like he'd never heard were whining past his ears then the minesweeper mounted the sand and the hull opened up as a whole invasion force of government soldiers poured up the beach to the palms. The soldiers had been hidden down there in their own vomit for a week. Then Brotherhood realised the whizzing past his red ears were bullets and he was viewed as part of the invasion force. "I thought you knew," the Captain said, crouched on the decking. "Welcome to Africa." '

'Caaan I?' the girl goes.

'You must ask Mother,' went the driver.

I says, 'Crossing The Interior to The Drome. What way?'

'Past the mud huts, try not to wake the baboons.'

'Byeee.' The little girl took away one hand to wave and the miniature train did a circle till its red light jerked and shaked away down the little track, its redness showing on the rails before it dived into a tunnel that seemed made of papier mâché. I trod on along the track, through the silly wee tunnel and round another bend. When I turned right onto open hillside the king baboons must've seen me cause they started such a commotion, and this in turn got all the bloody parrots along at the castle going bonkers.

Bended double like the clans at Culloden stepping into the end, I traversed bensides ever upwards. I climbed straight through steady blackout – the sodden Levi's going stiff on both thighs with the perishingness – knowing always, hung up in some place of aboveness like a cyan-coloured censer swinging in the wind, snugged up in the clam of a scree-clagged corrie, was the campfire: the campfire with its angle of floor that had let me see it when I swam out in the Sound but hid from view deep down at the sole bulb of Ferry Slipway below.

When I came on them it was sudden. The campfire lifted up out of the darknesses as I heave-heaved up a bank. I ducked down though I knew from the fire area, against nightsky, I'd be invisible.

Two guys – old, kind-of-harmless-looking-slack-jowelled-brotherly-baldiness made you trust them, as if one could never do anything bad in the always-look of his brother. But *it* was beyond them, *it* was lying within the light of the fair-old-bleeze. I squinted, made sure I was seeing what I was but I was so cold I stepped into their light and both men swung and looked at the coffin sitting beside them on the fold-down trestles before they bothered turn and begin to study me.

'Aye-aye,' coughs one of the brothers.

'Come away hence and form a square circle, girl.'

'Aye, let the dogs see the rabbit,' says the First Spoken.

'Where the hell've you been? Specting you for hours,' says the Most Baldy, pretend-annoyedly; he nicked a peek at First Spoken who let out a honky laugh.

'Busy the night.' (Gasped, glancing round.)

'Rush hour . . .'

'Off our feet . . .'

'Visitors are such a strain.'

I lowered myself beside the flames and looked into them, smiling; I announced: 'I cross the Interior to The Drome.'

'We go the other way. To open ocean. The three of us,' First Spoken spat into the fire. 'Guess what we've buried under that hearth? A fat clucky hen snaffled from old Gibbon's Acres wrapped in silver foil. Ready in . . .' (his watch clicked down as he flicked a wrist) . . . 'just a jiffy.'

'Know how to catch a chicken?' asked Most Baldy.

I goes, 'Nut.'

'You catch em at night,' cackled First Spoken.

'They cannae *see* in the dark!'

'Cannaesseeeeee!'

'Would you *like* a wee bite chicken?'

I goes, 'Oh *yess* I would. Yum-yummy.'

'Alexander. I hope you've polished the silver.'

'It was bloody parrot last night and never again.'

'Can I ask?' I looked across at the dark oak coffin on trestles.

'Scrawny creature. A parrot steak.'

'Dad,' nodded the First Spoken.

I nodded back.

'We promised him he'd be buried at sea . . .'

'And when he went from us a week on Tuesday we go and find you have to book *years* in advance for a burial at sea with the navy.'

'And him on the convoys all those years, is that not right, Alexander?'

'And of course *all kinds* of rules and red tape about doing your own bloody burial at sea . . .'

'Money makes no difference.'

' "Nae pockets on a shroud, boys." '

'That's what he always told us, "Nae pockets on a shroud," so we're burying him at sea ourselves, on the other side of the island; we have to cross to The Inaccessible Point, and cause it's inaccessible we have to take him in on foot.'

'And we'll need a boat to take him right out to sea when we get there . . .'

'Cast him off on the last voyage; right far out so the wood coffin doesnt float him back in . . .'

I says, 'Have you heard of a man called the Argonaut?'

'Him in the kayak? We couldn't trust Father to a one like yon.'

Just then a sound came from the coffin, I swung round towards it. It was coming from the insides of the coffin, it was the purrr, purrr, purrr of a cellnet phone.

'It's Dad's.'

'He asked to be buried with it . . .'

'He was very attached to it . . . never out of his right hand . . .'

'It's still in it . . .' the First Spoken muttered.

Most Baldy turned away from me to the First Spoken and went, 'That'll be old McKercher after his fee,' he looked at me and says, 'Our accountant.'

The phone stopped ringing and after a silence the First Spoken produced a packet of Chesterfields that he offered round. I shook head and goes, 'I've recently quit, thanks.' Most Baldy took and they lit up offof the fire. Some spits of rain started to come down.

'Contrary to speculation, *these* are what James Bond smoked,' goes the First Spoken.

The Second Spoken: Most Baldy, says, 'I am not James Bond nor was meant to be,' he stood and crossed over towards the coffin where a large sheet of polythene was folded; he picked it up and shook it out so's it made a big crackling noise. We were all looking over at the coffin: on its varnished side, bolted on, was a white metal plate with the black letters reflecting in the campfire's unsteady light:

'What's that number thing fixed to the side?' I goes.

'It's the personalised number plate from his Jaguar, there's the other on the opposite side.'

The Most Baldy draped the polythene over the coffin to protect it from the rain.

'Right, lets dig this chicken *up!*' goes the First Spoken. He took a stick and began shoving the red-hot cinders aside to get at the little oven he'd made in the soil under. Sudden, both men turned and looked out, towards the darkness of the Sound, then I heard it too, turned and saw the new light and the flashing red one too, moving: a cone of light pointing down and sweeping a sparkly circle over the waters.

'Nam the Dam, what's he doing?' the First Spoken moaned.

'The little ferry got sunk by the car ferry; there's a man missing.'

'It sunk? What *again!*' went the Most Baldy.

'That Nam the Dam shouldn't be out there, this is official.'

'He's an old yank from Vietnam with his own Westland Wessex. He lifts a lot of posts and wire when they're fencing high on the mountainsides. He does mountain and sea rescue in his spare time, it's bloody disgrace; you're a damn sight safer stuck on a rock face or floating at sea than you are in his old rust-bucket.'

I goes, 'Why's he got yon name?'

'Mind out now, lass, the Piston of Achnacloich's coming out. Come on now, son, out you come now, son'; the First

Spoken whipped out his knob and started doing just a massive number one on the flames of the campfire that hissed all wild; I jumped back from the balloons of steam and the old dangling doosey there as the smelly clouds lit up a bit then a last wet shadow flipped before all was pitch blackness.

The Most Baldy's voice went, 'Well. Guess we won't be eating that chicken.'

'They call him Nam the Dam cause he was a Huey pilot in Vietnam who spent twenty-five years recovering in Amsterdam before he came here.'

'If the lunatic sees us he'll come in and try to land; then he'll be all for lifting Father, flying him out to sea and dropping him from the helicopter.'

I says, 'Wouldn't that be more simple?'

'Lassie, lassie, you'll no understand how a Navy man won't let an airforce man into his business if he can help it.'

The voice of the Most Baldy went, 'Specially no some yankee with a long beard who's never seen shirt nor tie nor soap and water.'

We watched the searchlight from the helicopter patrol the Sound waters. It started to rain more, all the heavier.

Into the dark I says, 'Do either of yous know that guy, John Brotherhood, who has The Drome Hotel?' I could hear the raindrops patting on their plastic jackets. One coughed but I couldn't tell which. When one spoke it was the Most Baldy.

'We read Joseph Conrad; there's a bit where a girl is asked if she really believes in The Devil.'

The voice of the First Spoken says, 'She answers that there

are plenty of men worse than devils to make a hell of this earth.'

I slept under the coffin, the polythene flappered and the mobile phone inside the coffin got a couple of calls through the hours of darkness. I couldn't get to sleep as the slate-grey dawn of mists began. I crawled out letting the rain wash my face; I tiptoed past the tent and away round the sheep-paths and down into the first of the glens. Around midday I saw the bright yachting jackets high on the ridge above, moving towards the wide base of the telly aerial. In the distance, the multiple aerials of the old Tracking Station and Observatory: the upper structures of rusted satellite dishes lost in the mist or cloud.

I was so hungry I trembled when I stopped walking forwards so it was best just to press on. At the end of the glen, in the versant of the extinct volcano I came to the floor of moss, a-drip with water. Little droplets clinging to the frothy emerald and curly serrations of the lichen. My tongue flicked at the diamonds of liquid then my lips clamped onto the moss, by rubbing my face side to side with the base of my tongue right out I could gulp down gallons and taste the salady smeg of raw blossoming life. I could connect to our fetid origins in the faded, damp places. I found a pink growth and kneeled, my arse up in the air as I shoved my face deep-deeper into that planetary sponge of mossflowers, biting away at the base.

The cattledrovers seen me, bum in the air as they came down that old drove road. It was the stubbly Leader who

25

shouted, 'The moon's up already,' that got me turned round and on my feet like a shot.

You stared at the sight: the lazy swing of the cattle walk, with big diarrhoea splatters all up their shanks; there were one, two, three . . . eleven and the leading beast with its special coat all wet.

I crossed to the stubbly Leader guy, over the grass of the drove road that was so waterlogged it was reflecting the sky: I seemed to cross a floor of clouds towards him.

'Where are *you* headed?' he went.

'Drome over there.'

'There? We're headed landward to the Hinterlands. Today we've taken them over the Mist Anvils, skirted the Woodland Edges, now we're headed for The Far Places and we'll swim them over the Sound.'

'Never. Can cows swim?'

'They can swim *miles*,' the girl one with the video camera bawled.

'Long as you have a good lead beast the others follow,' says stubbly guy.

'You don't have an Ordnance Survey do you?' says the bearded, 'We're using this fifteenth-century one and it's loaded with inaccuracies.'

The girl one went, 'We're following the old black cattle-drove roads, come a hundred mile across Mainland.'

I held out my shaking arms, 'Whats all this for?'

'University project.'

'Some of the financial backing's EEC.'

'And a bit from the Arts Council . . .' the bearded one added.

'Keeping them all together at night's a hassle but we wanted to prove it could still be done,' girl one goes.

'Got anything to eat?' I came straight out with.

'Well, we've been doing hunting and fishing, trying to do the fifteenth-century thing with Gore-Tex and a video camera thrown in!'

The stubbly leader guy goes, 'We're just about to make camp down by the river though; we'll try a spot of night-fishing, bound to come up with something good.'

Second Night

In the sheer pitch dark over there I could hear the lead beast meandering, crunching out grass with those side-head jerks. The herd was tethered in black beyond where the bearded one was hunting with his fold-out crossbow. My bottom was saturated wet-through on the sodden grass by the campfire; suddenly old Last of the Mohicans stepped back into the wobbling shadows of the cast light. You noticed how he was smoking a joint, holding the crossbow by his thigh.

'How can you hunt at night?'

'Instinct,' he goes, then blethers on, 'In the Middle Ages they think all folk were permanently stoned from lysergic growths of roots in cereals: *everyone* wasted, dressing up animals in clothes and putting them on trial.'

Out of the darkness from the night-fishing came the stubbly Leader guy and the girl one with video camera. They had a coiled-up eel and a leaky bucket full of tadpoles. I wouldn't try the eel but the bearded one goes that it tasted a little like chicken. When they boiled the tadpoles each floated to the top of the bucket. The bearded one ate some then his face all curled up in the firelight. He picked up his crossbow then marched off till we couldn't hear him. When he returned he had a dead goose with an arrow in it. They chucked it all on the flames without even plucking, but it just went on fire, then exploded.

'Where's the lavvy?' I goes. Really meaning if they had any lavvy paper.

'Just go anywhere,' goes the girl one.

I gave her a look – her ladyship there – but she didn't have the gumption to cotton on. I walked and walked trying to get out of sight of the three of them round the campfire but you just couldn't tell at what bit they didn't see you any more. I cooried down and jobbied; the grass so wet it reflected the smeary line of campfire, the big blades of grass that I clutched and ripped out again and again to heave upward using both hands then toss away aside. It was the way life humiliated on top of everything: having to take a shit when you'd eaten nothing for forty-eight hours.

As I walked back towards the campfire you could see them, their pitch-black stick shapes, and I fell massively forward right over a black thing that rose up under rolling me to the side where my breath got knocked out and I swore in fright and clamped my arms over tum-tum; I curled, twisted head and looked into the face of the Devil, 'Brotherhood,' I whispered, then laughed out as I jamp to my feet so the breathing of the cow was at my chest; I gave out a wee yelp of scaredeyness then stepped backwards to see if the others had seen me do it.

I walked up to them and plonked myself down. 'Jesus, I'm famished,' I says.

'It's not just *you!*' the bearded one started howling and with a thung the crossbow at his thigh went off while I dived sideyways, holding myself away from the cinders' edges. We all heard the arrow hit, registered the pause, the ground shake out in the night; the first thump was the beast's knees coming down, the second big bump the body keeling side-wise.

Using a burning branch in his outstretched arm, the Leader led the way till we came to the carcass; the arrow had gone right in between its eyes.

'Jesus, the lead beast, you've gone and killed our lead beast, you crazy good-for-nothing.' The Leader shook his head. You could see the black blood in the hair on the dead cow's forehead, arrow stuck out.

'How are we going to lead them?' the girl one was going.

'The hell with that, lets roast this one,' I says. The other three stared at me in the burning torch-light over the black, wet carcass.

The Leader and the bearded one were eating with the dark blood still up to their elbows, fingers stuffing the thin meat strips into their mouths.

'I did a four-year stint in the Fleshers up at Far Places; that's how come I know these lands and I know your man Brotherhood at The Drome.' Leader chewed.

'I'm nothing to do with him, I've never met the guy.' I shook-shook my hand cause I'd burned my little finger on the hot meat again.

'Oh. You just don't look like one of the regulars at his hotel. I used to deliver the meat there. He would always collar you, y'know? This weird way of just launching in to stories, as if they were directed right at you; he wouldn't do it to me but I heard him doing it to the younger wives up in the Observation Lounge at nights, fire burning just like this – Brotherhood, the Sanctions Buster, trying to get a rise out the girls, talking *history*, his face just hidden, back in the shadows: ". . . so you're not familiar with that daughter? Her fate is well documented. I've researched it all. I used to be partial to a bit of research; the dusted golden bibliotheque light falling down on me, the worn desk, the place across from the main doors where I could take a café au lait and smoke a local brand. Ah, the daughter; she fell pray to the Parisian mob in that best studied of years for a little insight on human nature. 1789 and the mob had practised forms of revenge on their former oppressors, or shall we say tyrants, for what is life but a choice of tyrants and tyrannies? Anyway rape was very much in the air and this daughter, this particularly milky aristocrat, was cornered in her palace – some palace, I forget now and it doesn't matter anyway. You can imagine the cake those men made her eat after they tore away such fine silk and lace," and somewhere like here, Brotherhood would pause for effect, ". . . so fair her skin, some scholars have documented that even the women of the mob felt compelled to ride on her as sliding figureheads along with their men. To the universal disappointment of these avengers, the young girl fainted, or perhaps even died under their attentions so they dragged her into the courtyard where the servants and the girl's parents were standing, captured. In front of the eyes of the girl's mother and father, the revolutionary factor severed the head and limbs of the daughter. One seditionary lay the remaining torso before its mother and father, removed his breeches, found the torso's true part still intact and, in the firelight, to the howls of his comrades, that individual made a new kind of love to the headless, legless, armless trunk. Imagine the scene if you will! When he stood up grinning at the mother, the blood that coated him would have glistened black in the hand-held torch-light and the flames of the now-burning palace. Not content with this, though, our children of the revolution loaded an old cannon with gunpowder and fired the severed head, each limb and finally the violated torso, against a stone wall next to the mother and father who were forced to watch. The mob then subjected the parents and the entire household to the dismemberment and cannonball-express treatment."

'Out of the semi-darkness around the Observation Lounge fireplace, punctured by the intensifying then politely manoeuvring cigarette tips, one of the young wives' voices spoke:

' "But that was so long ago . . ."

'Brotherhood's voice speaks, after a throaty, experienced chuckle, "I lied."

' "About what they did to that girl?" the youngest wife, the non-smoking one whose veins show around her temples in the light at breakfasts, the grey light of a universe that doesn't know how to stop existing, that hums in the Observation Lounge window, sickly in its monotony: a jellyfish light trembling off the Sound waters.

'Brotherhood spoke, "No. All these things did happen, I

just changed the date and a few details. Everything I describe happened in Europe. Last year." The Sanctions Buster sniggered in the darkness.'

The cattledrovers had no tents, they'd been wrapping themselves in animal skins bought at an upholsterer's, except the bearded one who slept high in a tree to escape floodwaters. I put on the extra yacht jacket and pulled up both hoods tight, using the clothes in the kitbag as a pillow, I got a better night's sleep than underneath that coffin the night before. When it was still dark I was taken out of doziness by the strangest patrolling lights across the glen floor. I wasn't that sure if what I'd seen had been a dream or actual – the movements of the queer shadows – so I turned my head, looking over the gone-out fire towards the river. I saw a little island, its black base by the lit-up water, the twigs and branch clumps so thick you couldn't see through; the topmost whorls of black twigs were burning, the water-line wood giving out smoke wisps as the whole contraption was floating downriver, casting its light on either bank till it moved way down the glen.

Third Night

It was earlier in the day I had seen the horse. I had been moving along the glen floor then, way in the distance, seen the big horse walking towards me. It was one of those shire things: had a harness round its neck and gave me the filthiest look as it headed off, breaking into a trot now and then. I stood looking round but there wasn't a soul.

That night I sighted a chain of burnings all the way down the next glen, the flames reflecting on the black water of the river, running away like a flow towards the coastline. I imagined a convoy of the burning clumps drifting, but the longer I looked I realised the burning islands in the river were not moving along the river's length.

'Charlie!'

I heard him calling up ahead before I saw his torch-light and stepped off the track.

'Charlie!'

You felt kind of sorry for him so I called out of the woods, 'Is it a horsey you're looking for?'

You saw the guy go all agog, rooted to the spot and

slashing the beam of his torch left and right then shield his eyes. I stepped out, his beam jittered across to me, shimmied up and down my body then it clicked off. 'Jesus,' he goes, under the breath, then, 'What are you *doing* out here at night?'

'Know The Drome Hotel?'

'Brotherhood's place? You trying to get there or more like get away from it?'

'I'm *going* there.'

'You seen that bastard Charlie?'

'The horse? I saw a big horse early the day but it was way miles back in the last glen.'

'Oh Christ, what way was he headed?'

'To the coast and going like the clappers.'

'Damn him, he thinks he's still on Mainland. Every Friday he's on the dot at five, buggerlugs, he knows when to knock off so he just starts for home, won't do a stroke of work after five. It was old Charlie got the train derailed back on Mainland: got stuck at the level-crossing with a load of logs behind him, train came along, crashed over the logs and off the track, old Charlie just walked on home to his stables easy as you like.'

'What is it that's going on here; all those . . . bonfires right up the river?'

'We're contract loggers, thirty men clearing the wood up above the big house; those fires you see, it's the rock outcrops along the river. With all the sneddings and wastewood we burn the rocks at night to break them up, then we dynamite in the morning and clear the stone; we're trying to deepen the river, so we can float the logs right out of the Interior and downriver towards The Drome to barge them away up Sound.'

I came straight out with, 'Got anything to eat?'

'Look, those guys here, theyre a bit girl-mad, you know, all they're after right the now is a bit of Up the Klondike to Bangalore with a wee touch of ginger; an innings, a game set and match finished off with a full flavoured robusta ... y'know what I mean?'

'Aye.' I goes.

'I just don't think you should go marching in.'

He paused then he goes, 'Let's see you closer up. You from The Island?'

'Nut.'

'Why you headed Brotherhood's way? That mother won't let us pick up the logs at the river mouth by The Aerodrome there ... he wants a cut o' the money.'

'Why shouldn't I be? Why's everyone so scared of Brotherhood, he's no the bogeyman is he?'

'He's killed people, in Africa and two young girls from just the next glen here.'

'How do you know he's killed people? He'd be locked up.'

'He didn't axe them or anything, but he might as well have.'

'What happened?'

'What's your name?'

'My name?' I tried to decide. Lynniata, or Serenella Cerano Berniez or other of the names that I'd used to amuse me. In the end it was my own name I spoke out and that he spoke back, the vowels pushing from the end of his lips as he seemed to stand on tiptoe, face unseen.

'Food. Look around your feet _____' (and here he said my name) . . . 'you're in the land of milk and honey.'

I looked down at the deep shadows by my boots, the splurge of his torch-light flittered around my toe-caps, then I picked out a scattering of shining, gold-coloured tins, flat ones with curvy edges; I cooried and picked one up.

'Rations, probably dumpling or, if youre lucky, boiled sweeties. Army rations nicked off the Territorials. This guy called Nam the Dam, sort of drunk who flies a helicopter, he's doing the provisions drops every week but he's some crazies on board that're tipping out the boxes all over the hillside; we're walking miles finding cans scattered all over the shop.'

You opened the can with a key, like a Spam can and it was dumpling inside that I ate with the edge of the guy's knife. We sat down against a tree trunk while the guy smoked a cigarette.

'Know how these hills were planted with forestry?' he goes.

In between chomps of the dumpling I goes, 'Nut.'

'Old Bultitude had these cannon. Old gunpowder ones, back in the fifties he had them dragged up the glen here, then they spent days shooting canisters of spores and seedlings at the mountainsides.'

I nodded, thought of Brotherhood's story of cannon. There was only the inhale-glow from the guy's ciggy that lit up his deep eye-sockets.

He whispered, 'Know why we're chopping down the forest? Eldest son from the Big House at the bottom of the glen shot himself up here last year, blew his brains all over a rowan tree. The old lady up at the house looks out onto this forest from her bedroom. She shifted rooms in the big house but whenever she saw the wood it reminded, so . . . we're to chop the whole thing down and burn every trace of it. I'm up here with Charlie. Some of the slopes are so steep you can never dream of getting a tractor up, so we haul all the lot out with Charlie and his spinnel. I'm normally planting the trees so it feels bad, but a lux penny is a lux penny.'

'Look, I'm meaning nothing by it, but can I lean my head against your shoulder?' I says.

He goes, 'Course. Aye, have a wee snooze.'

In the dark I went, 'Did Brotherhood really kill girls?'

Speaking, so's his shoulder trembled nicely against my cheek he says, whisperly, 'It's so warming that you trust me here: a girl in woods at darkness looking as divine as you . . .'

I bumped my ear on his shoulder in the laugh . . . 'Divine!!!'

'. . . Come striding out of the dark East with some water stars over your shoulder. I mean I'm not after you or anything.' He breathed in all excited and says, 'Do you believe in poetic moments? I believe that's what happiness is: trying to live a succession of poetic moments, not stuck in the Portakabins with that lot but out, under the last trees, meeting a tall crazy girl . . . watching the sunrise in a stranger's arms.'

'Hey. I'm not crazy.'

'. . . 'Magine a life that is one long poem . . .'

'. . . I'm moving off before light but can I put my arm round here. I just need to cuddle . . .' The shoulder shook.

'I'm married and I love her. Is this being bad?'

I goes, 'This is not being bad; I bet she's dead lovely.'

'When she smiles she frowns at the same time. She used to work up at the old tracking station where the Observatory was. It was summer, she undressed so slowly outside it was dark before she drew her tights down and with a match she showed me the faint mole on her thigh that corresponded exactly with the shape of the star cluster she'd been studying. Her mobile phone went off but she left it in the grass somewhere and I knew as we kissed she was really trying to remember my name from back at the party, saying she didn't care where her life went. When she lay back she lost who I was forever, mumbling the names of the blue stars above us.'

After a good bit I says, 'It must be so lovely to be like that.'

'Ho, here's me and a girl I've knowd a half-hour with her arm round me . . .'

'It doesnt count,' I says, 'Believe me, mister, I want you to love her *more*. I want you to say hello. I've kicked myself free the earth long ago . . . I don't count.'

'Aye? A blow-jobbing's out the question then?'

We both laughed and a bird crashed free of the drooping umbrellas of pine branches, shaking so much waterdrops out, the canopy of twigs swung back up all the higher.

Out of the nightness he says, 'It'll happen to you too.'

'What?'

'The Love.'

39

'Nah. There was someone once but, never the right person since . . .'

'It'll come, it'll come like a disease.'

'No.'

There was long long quietness.

'Look at the stars; this world so big and just us here,' he went.

I goes, 'Brotherhood?'

'The Erin sisters it was, from over at The Summer Colony between the Bird Sanctuary and The New Projects. It was after Brotherhood came back in that old plane. He made them both fall in love with him. Made them. With his handsomeness and money. His father was working like a slave at The Drome Hotel while Brotherhood gallivanted around these hills with Lynne and Rosa in his jeep. He took them in the flying boat, flew them up the coast, low over the Summer Colony chapel, over the beaches at The Inaccessible Point, the birds from the Sanctuary peeling off the cliffs below the tilted wings: puffins and shags dropping straight to the sea. I can just imagine the Erin sisters, who we all felt protective about, noses pressed to the windows.

'I was just out school then and would slouch at one end of the public bar at The Drome, 'fore Brotherhood the younger shut it down, making the bar resident only; there he would be, proudly laying off about it in a loud whisper, the stories that he still repeats, word for word to the young wives beside the evening log-fires in the Observation Lounge.'

'What stories would he tell?' I mumbled, sleepy sort of.

'All of his going with the sisters.'

'Let me guess: he *went* with them *both* thegether, he climbed into the same bed with them or they came into the same bed with him for some triple action? Big deal. I've done worse.'

He spoke out, 'Well yes. Of course.'

'That's no so naughty; just being first to do it in Toytown.'

'Aye, but its not like you think. Brotherhood, up in the bar would tell, his face back in the shadows: "I can remember it was Lynne I kissed first. The three of us sitting up on the banks of Sorrowless Rigs Burn. An August afternoon. As Lynne's mouth and mine came together she lay back under me. My hand went to her right leg and I still recall its teenage-smoothness. Rosa, who had put her head back at the same instant on the heather let out a gasp." Same words as he'll use on the young wives up at the Observation Lounge who'll be sitting, legs crossed, as Brotherhood looks into their eyes, watching as the women think . . . *he's completely insane. We've put ourselves into the hands of a psychopath for a fortnight* . . . Brotherhood scans, looking for any sign of arousal in the women; he goes on . . . "Lynne and I moaned, but so did Rosa. As I kissed Lynne her sister was moaning! As I rubbed higher on the leg," (And here Brotherhood might lean closer in the semi-dark lounge.) ". . . I found Lynne was letting me move up under the dress; my fingers brushed over the belly-button and up to a tit. Lynne was gurgling in her throat as my fingers found, on the tip of the left nipple, a single hair." (Now, Brotherhood is getting into his stride.) "Between thumb and forefinger, I pinched the single hair and ran my fingers down it to judge its length and – amazing – that

41

incredible hair stretched on and on from the nipple, one foot, two feet, three feet long, it led my hand across to where it ended: the silver ring of the pierced nipple on Rosa's equally smooth breast. Now Rosa was breathing so hysterically; there was the delight and fascination of discovering where Lynne's sensations ended and Rosa's began and I never really defined it that day. Looking into the twins' faces, their thin noses and black eyes, telepathic lovers co-operating for the pleasure of us all, as I slid a hand to the side of the third leg and judged that ultimate point; felt for the wonder of that same wet confirmation a man to the east of Europe had felt for, as he lay a-top the bag of blood that was a slim young woman minutes before – what his hand found was what mine did, that common bit, that secret where the twins truly shared everything and I entered their single vagina, I loved them. Other men were too afraid; though I wasn't the first. Look at the wives of The Bunker Twins. The Bunkers were not critically joined like Lynne and Rosa, who shared a bladder, a digestive system, reproductive organs. The Bunker Twins were brought together by a fatty phalanx of skin along their sides. Two sisters married them and between them, in nights of mutual passion, they fathered twenty children, all healthy. They lived to the ripe old age of seventy-three, each dying on the same night." '

I whispered, 'Siamese twins, the Erin sisters were Siamese twins.'

'That's right. Brotherhood installed them in the hotel until he'd driven both women mad with jealousy for each other. Rosa tried to hack Lynne apart from her with a carving knife; they bled to death during the airlift.'

'He would go to bed with them and they were joined up?'

'They only had one . . .

I goes, 'Jesus.' I'd taken my head off his shoulder.

He went, 'You can imagine what gossip has been echoing round the island. There's always a physically dominant twin; when they were children it was always Lynne who limped forward, dragging that third leg behind them. There's tragedy written into those dynamics and Brotherhood just had to exploit it to set them against each other.'

'What's all this about young wives in the hotel he speaks all these stories out to?'

The guy lit another cigarette, offered, and I shook head. 'Guests. He runs The Drome Hotel as a honeymoon place. It's all done through travel agents in the Central Belt: couples get flown in on these light aircraft; Brotherhood picks them up in this crazy white limo with pink interior, they stay a fortnight and get the wee plane out again. Crazy scene.'

I'd put the head back down on his shoulder and I know he was talking, warning me, but I nodded off.

I came awake. I thought he'd gone then saw the glow of a cigarette over by a tree. My cheek was resting on his rolled-up jacket, the cold zip dugged into my cheek.

'Yup.'

'Hiya.'

'You were talking in your sleep.'

I smiled, breathed out warm air from my nose.

'You says, "Brotherhood," and another name too, and he says the name I didn't recognise until later, and that was

43

impossible for me to know then, but truly that is what he said as if all that happens has already. Light was jumping up behind the looming mountains further into the Interior and I was bye-bidding the night-talker and lashing on past the portakabins and into more mysteriousnesses of mist banks, darkness, the lantern sky behind and gold embers of islets strewn along the river with burn-out smoke rising in the cold dawning air, making the waterway look on fire.

Sun was up and I was near one of the Backroads when I heard the explosions up the glen, then it was feet onto the slap of tar road and on down until the purr of Knifegrinder's motorcycle coming up from the rear.

'Man, you are zilch, you are zilch in weirdyness to things I did and saw way Down There,' I shouted at him as he approached, the stag's horns on his motorcycle helmet (that he was later arrested for as an accident hazard) moving slow from side to side as he braked to a stop; the old motorbike phutting away.

'Want any knives sharpened?' he goes, produced a crab apple from his biker jacket and stuck it up onto an end spike of the antler horns. He growled, shook his head till the apple flew off and rolled a bit down the road. He took out the bird-noise whistle he used outside the kitchens, sculleries and shops to tell of his arrival; he blew its weird whirling sound.

'I don't have a knife.' Then my mind jumped and my fingers found the forester's knife in the yachting jacket's pocket. 'Well I've this . . .'

'*Nice* piece . . .'

'It's not even mine. Got any food?' I walked to the apple,

picked it on up and without rubbing it on the Levi's, I bit into it. I goes, 'Look,' hoiked the knapsack off and took out the other yacht jacket from the Chandlers, offering it. 'Give us a backie over to The Drome Hotel.'

'Aye. Lost your husband?'

'I just want to stay there a bit.' I looked up at the awful hugeness of mountain tops round us. 'Then everything will be alright again. For a while.'

He took the jacket in his hands then handed it back, 'Not my style, honey.'

'You could sell it on.'

'Tell you what, I'll sharpen your knife for nothing!' He wheeched his leg sudden over the bike so's you had to take a step back to mind the antlers. With a squat he was down lifting the bike onto its fold-out stand, then he took a belt, like a Hoover belt, attached it to a grooved disc by the centre of the back wheel; from a worn leather pannier he took a black grinding stone with its glistening wee bits, and affixed it near the pedal, pulled on the belt taut, and when he turned the throttle on the handlebar the stone went whizzing round.

'It's okay. Really,' I says.

'Give it here; I'll give it a dicht.' He took the knife and began the folding out of some blades from the handle. There was a wee set of scissors that he squinted at then began snipping away at the bushy nostril hairs peeking out of his nose. 'I'll give you a hurl for this.'

'It's no mine. It's a friend's and I'll need to give it back.'

With both hands he pushed the little blade onto the spinning stone, a screeling noise hurled sparks down onto the

45

wet macadam. Very handily he flipped the knife over and leaned in the blade again. 'Do you know Chef Macbeth at The Drome? I do all his knives for him.'

'I don't know anyone there.'

'Why are you going?'

'Wee holiday,' I shrugged shoulders.

'Huh! That'll be right.'

I says, 'Mmm, is it all guests are husband and wife – new, like?'

'Nah – nah, they've that Man From The Department of Transport. You'll see him. You'll see that one thieving all the bits of sheds and outhouses back; it's legal landfall, legitimate salvage, I was talking about this with the Argonaut. It's legitimate salvage, girl!'

Just to be on the safe side I took the knife off him. Sudden-like he had the buttons on his shirt undone and was tugging it open so's you could see the greying hairy chest. I took a few steps away.

'I've a hole in the heart. Listen! Boom-boom BOOM, boom-boom BOOM! Listen, girl.'

'Don't really want to.'

'Listen for luck.'

I huffed out a puff and swept my hair, that was heavy and greasy, away from my ear, leaned down and ever so cautious-like put my side of face against the hard chest. It was right enough, the heart beat weirdly with a third beat added on strangelike. 'You're right enough, your heart beats differently,' I took my head up and shook my hair.

Knifegrinder leered, 'Some of us beat to a different drum.'

'Aye. That much is true,' I says.

He buttoned up his shirt and started to sing or shout:

'Mama she was the work of the Devil
And the fire escapes are burned to Hell...'

He walked in a circle pretending to play guitar then he rapidly scuffled over and up to my face hissing, '*You* know fine why you're here and so do I, Jessie, youre a hunter and scavenger like the rest that come here from all ends of the galaxy. A hunter with a wee goal in mind, eh, EH! Well I'll tell you something, I'll tell you something, Calamity Jane,' he swung his head in all directions scanning the hillsides that were leaping up all round us with white gashes of new-filled streams striping the glen among the wet, green knobbles and bracken spreads of tan, 'I've *seen* it girl, I've seen it... SEEN! I've... I have touched it,' he whispered. 'Wreckage part of alien spaceship.'

'Right.' I goes.

'Brotherhood let me.'

'Aye?'

'Aye. AYE, of course aye. I saw what it did. Oh man, Oh MAN, you can not understand, you cannot comprehend it, everything you believed turning to powder in your hands, in these hands. IT.'

I nodded and made to be walking on up the glen. He walked after me.

'Brotherhood let me. Brotherhood *likes* me. Mr Brotherhood to you. It was him gave me my horns here. I was with him in the Land Rover. We'd dugged a big pit and that stag just fell in the hole. Couldnt get the big devil out so Brotherhood flung a noose round his neck, tied it onto the Land Rover and, well, y'know, just drove off. Man, you shoulda seen that porker's eyes bulge, his neck snapped and he bounced up. Hardy thing was still alive, so Mr Brotherhood ties a rope up to a tree then stretches that stag out with the Land Rover in second gear; puts on the gas and rrrrrip, spine and a balloon of intestines, the head tears off. I was happy with that but Brotherhood kept tethering up bits of the beast, gralloching a leg out the socket then leaping out the Land Rover, striding back and hooking up to the rib-cage or whatever, tearing the thing to pieces, blood up his arms, fat bluebottles oozing over everything. I tell you there's no rules binds that man to the earth.'

I'd been looking at the ground.

'Sure there's nothing else you want sharpened? I've done lady nail-files before; yon wee metal ones yous carry as weapons.'

'Don't have one.'

'Hell, there was a boy came stumbling out the bushes back there with bow and arrows, wanted them sharpened when he saw what I was; man, I'm such a dab hand with that wheel I could sharpen your pencil if you had one.' He walked back to his bike and started dismantling the gear, kicked it off its stand and accelerated up behind so's I stepped aside into the grass.

He braked beside me and pointed straight up the mountain to the behind of me. 'You'd be the quickest trotting over yon and falling down onto the foothills behind; keep a mile this side of the river and move west, it'll take you right into The Drome.'

As I climbed I kept the turning to watch the little bike move down the glen, Knifegrinder not tilting into the corners but taking them weirdly upright, so slow he seemed as to have stopped on the corners but no, he was moving on forwarders then suddenly really sped up on a fast bit of straight.

I moved into the lashing of mist among the scattered rocks, level sections of tuft grass broadened out then hoiched up onto another flanker. Peewee nests were a-clutter; mummy birds swooped down yelling at me and another did the old hop-along pretending to have a broken wing to lure me away from the nest – tenderly I stepped over the near-invisible tawn circles with the tiny yellow and brown eggs.

Higher near ridge-crest, the rondel trees of the valley floor clustered closer into mushy clumps of black with bumpy edges. The whole island seemed to slip down through me like a disc, spread out round, saw otherside from up there, distant mountains lifting up as if explosions of steam, cloud pillars like spring blossom, the mountain range I was named after on the opposite side of the Sound that lay with a wet sun along in dazzling shimmers, up to where the water turned angry black – wide wide ocean that goes forever 'cept maybe for a Pincher Martin rock jutted out the teeth of ocean bed. I stood looking out into that sea that surrounded us.

Weeks later up in the Observation Lounge it was the thought of our entrapment by water that got me talking about The Rudder Feeling. I was sat with the short skirt on, the tops of my thighs thinning as they dove into the hem I'd just cut, under the bewildered gaze of new-husbands and suspicious new-wives; I'd mesmerised them: the tale of my arrival at the London airport with my lipstick all snogged off as I walked along those millions miles of corridors and through customs in bare feet with just a plastic bag of dirty knickers; strapped on my back a huge teddy bear that'd been won me at the shows in, maybe Formentera maybe Fuerteventura, who knows? I was laughing, my black eyes averted, laughing for myself alone – at least one-time joys insured forever, even against that perilous stay in Brotherhood's sphere. I says, 'Rudder Feeling is very different from Toffee Feeling. The Rudder Feeling is when I was wee my foster-dad would hold my hand and take me to see the fishing boats. I'd no interest in boats, only in the textures and sizes of their rudders and propellers that I could see hung in the bluey-green world below the curves of the hulls. It gave me scaredness lying in my bed thinking about those rudders, held there forever, punished above the cold Atlantic seabeds that were always rolling out below them.'

The Aircrash Investigator, The One Who Walked the Skylines of Dusk with Debris Held Aloft Above His Head, HE nodded quick, several times, the whisky jamp up the insides of his tumbler and he says, 'You fear underworlds where the seabed is the earth, the unsteady surface a new sky, you hate the Living Things: basking shark or angler fish that might brush against you bare leg and those rudders and propellers . . . their contant immersion, made them thresholds into that underworld.'

He was right. I nodded watching as his faraway eyes turned to the gunmetal of the Soundwaters.

That was all later though; before my Banishment, so I clambered on up the steepening braes till all the island was way below me and I was dropping through the grey seams of sideyways rock – some cliffs were too sheer so's you had to make the big detours and wind down into the foothills below, using the sheep tracks.

I saw the tent way back on the lee dip in 96-Metre Hill, the oily tong of smoke crawling up above the larch scatterings. Even a real ways off you could pick out his bulk afront the tent.

'Ahoy there,' I waved.

'Well. Venus on the Half-Shell,' the Devil's Advocate shouted, his voice carrying a little away with the smoke from his campfire.

'I'm so so sorry; the petrol, in that tank. You could easy of died.' I walked up to quite near him.

'Sit down, dear, sit down. I'll tell you this, I was instrumental in the recent demotion of St Christopher from his position: patron saint of wayfarers.'

'Aye. I know,' I goes.

'Well! He certainly wasn't on board our vessel that night.'

'Thats right enough. They were searching for you. In a helicopter.'

'Worry not. I met two Mormons crossing these hills to The Far Places on their mission from Salt Lake City, Utah.

The gentlemen informed me a search had been called off. A reward has been posted for an escaped bear and that helicopter's esteemed crew are scouring the hills for the grizzly.'

'From the zoo at the castle?'

'The same.'

'This island is crazy. Its all like a dream.' I looked at the Devil's Advocate's face. It had the same similarities as all the other menfaces I'd been seeing.

'Where is it you wayfare to?'

'The Drome Hotel. That's a great tent you've there,' I says.

'So. Mr Brotherhood's lair.'

'Is it far?'

He went, 'Just beyond those trees.'

I stood, leaving the knapsack, then ambled over to the larch trees. Below me lay the wide waters of the Sound; the graveyard surrounded by the rivulets of the river outflow; the bright green of the airstrip threshold; the grass runway behind the pine plantation; the Big Road and, there, in among the pines, the roofs and angles of The Drome Hotel and outhouses.

I sauntered back to the wee camp. The Devil's Advocate was breaking off specks of loaf and tossing them in front of him. As I got closer the fat man turned to me and mouthed shushness. I spotted the robin redbreast bobbing on the mossy log and saw the two total black beads of its eyes.

The Devil's Advocate goes, 'They say the robin tried to remove the crown of thorns from Christ's head; the blood stained the bird's chest.'

I went, 'Is that right? You couldn't spare some of that loaf could you?'

He looked at me closely and held out the bread so's the robin redbreast dove off thanklessly, ducking and rising away over tubular hulks of mossed-out tree trunks long-fallen on the spongy hillside.

'Ta.' I screwed off a chunk of bakery loaf and held out the remaining back to him. He lowered those eyes, the whites so clear you'd think he had make-up round the skin. He looked back at my must've-been-black eyes; narrowed his own.

'You don't look well.'

'I'll be fine when I get to the hotel.' I saw him look me up and down and somehow, I knew he knew right there and then.

'Sit down here by the fire.' He stood and shifted off the log that he'd cleared the moss from and must've been sat on so much the wood was dry and smooth. I put my arse on it and bit away the rest of the loaf.

'I've tinned soup, tinned peaches cold down in the burn there. Join me?'

I nodded quick.

He walked towards the rushing sound of the river then turned back to look at me. 'The Just for the unjust, that He might bring us to God. Peter. Chapter 3. Verse 18.'

'Mmm. Uh-huh,' I nodded, chomping on the bread.

Split-second he sunk beneath the hill buff I whipped round and stuck my head in the tent. It smelled of sweat, there were lots books, a big crumpled-up sleeping bag in the strange blue light caused by the tent fabric. A big backpack leaned against the zipper door. I fiddled with the side pockets, looked back over my shoulder and tried another then scuffled forwards, keeping muddy boots off things. As a pillow, he was using a rolled-up towel that was damp; I reached in for a wallet and moment I touched it I knew what it was.

When he rolled back up the hill I saw him spit the butt of a fag out then wave the cans joyously.

'Brotherhood who owns The Drome, there seems to be a lot of crap talked about him,' I says.

'John Brotherhood.' He nodded, pretending to chew something, swinging round and dumping more branches on the fire, letting twigs brush against my feet threateningly. 'You've changed your jacket,' he smiled.

'This is my old favourite. Yon other one, I got after the wee ferry sunk. We all got free clothes from the Chandlers there. You should've seen it. How did you get ashore safe?'

'It was a miracle,' he smirked, both dirty hands held up. He produced a cigar from inside his cassocky thing, kneeled and, twirling the cigar, heated it on the new flames. 'You always warm a good cigar so it burns evenly and . . .' he nicked the end with good white teeth then, looking vulnerable, he trembled on his knees holding the cigar in his mouth, 'You must *never* let the flame you light with touch the cigar, or you can ruin the whole flavour; you light a cigar on the heat that rises above the flame. Listening?' he says, outright scary now.

'Know what kind of cigarettes James Bond smokes?'

'Sure. What makes you mention James Bond?'

'*What* then?'

'Chesterfields.'

'Is James Bond a saint?'

He'd got the cigar lit and laughed out really loud at me, 'A confessor if ever there was one! Dear, he might be the only one we've got on this earth.'

'You really do what the Harbour guy says back at the sinking? Eh . . . says you were a decider, who should be saint and that.'

'Thats exactly what I do.'

I nodded. There was silence. We stared at each, then I broke it by reaching in and taking out the penknife. 'It's got a can opener.'

'I've got my own.' He took out a knife and started digging in to the can top. 'I was in Mexico recently.'

'Oh aye?'

'Yes. There had been reports of a miracle. I was sent to investigate. A rural area. The face of Christ was appearing as an apparition on the outside wall of a little chapel. I arrived there on a Sunday to find the crowds gathered and on their knees before the south wall and I could see it too . . .'

'You could see?'

'Oh yes. I saw it. The face of the Saviour: the beard, the cheekbones from Golgotha. So I waited until midnight; myself and the priest went out with buckets and water, swept down the whitewash on the wall . . .'

'And . . .'

'It became evident the local farmers had been praying to a poster for a 1973 Willie Nelson concert in the next big town.'

55

I looked at him and burst out in the hysterics. He smiled, then laughed too. He tipped the soup into a very new-looking pan with wee fold-out handle, wrapped his hand in a cloth then held the pan in the flames. 'Look,' he nodded.

The sun was well down the far end of the Sound, the mountains sloping out of the shores on each side; along the ridge of the next hill, across the river, fairly sloping down to the verge of the big road, moved the figure, silhouette cut out against the light to the behind. The legs feeling their way, they juttered forward gingerly; arms shakily erect, holding the wide, flapping piece of whateverness above, held there cause too big for under-arm. He moved on, casting his own shadow over the dead bracken spreads; if you had to imagine the right music for the sight of him moving across the skylines it might be Stone Temple Pilots doing Big Empty offof The Crow soundtrack or if you had to choose a Verve song you'd obviously go for something offof the first album, Slide Away would be best.

The Devil's Advocate went, 'A resident from The Drome Hotel.'

'Friend of Brotherhood's?' I squinted into the afternoon.

'From what I've heard. Those are bits of two aircraft that crashed on the airfield ten years ago. This one here, who collects all the pieces, arrived a few months ago from the Department of Transport. Apparently they've re-opened the case. He's living in the hotel amongst all those horrible couples, investigating why the two planes collided; just little planes but two men were killed.'

I took the soup and ate it out the pan with a spoon. It was

too hot, though, so I rested it on my knees and watched the figure of The Aircrash Investigator with his burden, vanishing among the hillshadow. I says, 'In the nineteen-seventies, was it guns and stuff Brotherhood was selling way over in other countries?'

'Yes. And unrepentantly from that school that if he didn't sell the goodies to them the next man would. I used to know young Brotherhood. He once told me of some war – there were so many – and the airforce managed to get fuel but they had no weapons left at all: no rockets, no bombs, not even bullets for machine guns. Brotherhood presumed there would be no airforce attacks but there were: the jets came in low and very fast over civilian villages. The pilots emptied bags of rusty nails out the open cockpits. "Nails travelling at 300 m.p.h. can make quite a decoration on a child's body," those were Brotherhood's words. It's unusual. He never shows any feelings yet it was clear the day made a hefty impression on him. He said that was when he understood the Devil had won the struggle one day no one noticed; we're just under the impression the struggle still goes on. For him that was the day he realised all men dream of the nuclear explosion when they make love and secretly crave the destruction of their own children out of curiosity. Love was a petty illusion and he made it his business to show love existed nowhere in the world. That is why he set up this ludicrous honeymoon hotel; he likes the vulgarity of it and amuses himself searching for the proof he always finds, showing none of the couples is truly in love . . .'

'But love does exist; only yesterday . . .'

'I wish you could prove it to Brotherhood. He's a man who will not allow himself a single illusion.'

'I can't imagine your calling impresses him much then.'

He chuckled, 'He's no fan of me. You think I work with illusions? Think what happened after they put your man up on that cross?'

'He's never helped me once,' I goes, then went beetroot as I suddenly realised the soup was finished and I'd already stolen from this man. He took back and handed me the opened peaches.

'Watch you don't cut your tongue.'

'I've never tasted anything so sweet,' I smiled at him. He nodded and carried on smoking his cigar.

'What *are* you? Some kind of a drifter?' he goes.

'I been travelling here and there,' I says. 'You're no going to tell me I should be settled.'

'That's a matter for your . . .' he blew out a splut of smoky laugh.

I gulped and nodded, trying to swallow the peaches down. I says, 'Tell us another Brotherhood story then I'm off to kiss the shite's arse.'

'Look. I don't know your game down there but you don't strike me as the typical treasure hunter.'

'What do you mean, sunken treasure like yon Argonaut's hunting?'

'Mmm. No . . .'

'What then?'

'What's your business down there?'

'Personal.'

'You could step into crossfire.'

'There's no need to go the all-dramatic on me.'

'Brotherhood'll chew you up: a girl looks like you,' he laughed; shook his head, 'I'm crazy to even consider letting you go down that hill.'

I stood quick, picked up the kit-bag, holding it up to my chest, the side with the patch on it facing away from me. The Devil's Advocate stayed put as I started to stroll away from the fire.

'On you go. I can't help it, I just thought you were more than another who wanders these demented lands in days of the end.'

'Aye, but its always the days of the end for yous bible-bashers; thats all we've ever heard from you.'

'If you think about it, girl, every day is the end for someone and will be here soon enough for you.'

'Lighten up, man,' I says as I crested 96-Metre Hill. 'Thanks for the food.'

I kept on down that wide slope in the failing light; only later I would see that the one known as The Devil's Advocate had turned back to his tent, checked under the pillow and saw what he'd suspected; let out his wholesome laugh. He could easy have shouted, started running down the hill and caught me before I'd crossed the first of the barbed-wire fences, but I was believing myself off, striding into the duskness, the kit-bag pushed out before me like a pregnancy, knowing all the time how

[Editor's note: three words
illegible; possibly *Villian once says*]

SECOND MANUSCRIPT
Part One

Saturday the Fourteenth

I was in the Observation Lounge above the grass runway and I saw her figure hugging a kitbag on 96-Metre Hill to the south of the hotel and airstrip. She appeared beside the stunted larch: the larch on which, reposing, but ruined by hoody crows and hostile weather, the pilot's corpse had been found ten years before.

That evening on which she appeared was clear and bitter cold. The convoy (some cars with headlights already on) from the vehicle ferry had already moved along the big road on the shoreline towards The Outer Rim.

I had an unobstructed view of her distant figure moving downhill off the slopes, striding through the gloaming of dying sun that lit the tangled spreads of fallen bracken alternately rust then scarlet in colour; the inverted stalks washed and battered to an earth that would be a hard grid of frost under the coming dark.

For an instant, above the shoreline, the newcomer's figure was silhouetted along with the farthest larch-outcrops that are scattered on the bare hills above the hotel and airstrip. The silver-grey light on the water of the so-called bay stopped sparkling. The sun moved down behind the snow-capped mountains that form the far shores of the Mainland along the fjord-like Sound.

She came down onto the shoreline close to the chapel ruins and graveyard where the remains of the pilot lay buried. The light was failing badly when she next materialised on the hotel side of the pine plantation that obscured the far end of the runway and its southern threshold, above which the aluminium folded together ten years ago in the darkness. She must have traversed the machair which, in the coming flush we dared call Spring, would blot with pure white daisies: an expanse that would turn pink as a cold cloud passed over and the sensitive under-petals, that looked as if they'd had a little burgundy spilled on them, turned up in resignation. She used the roadbridge to cross the river which was in spate, pulling down tonnes of freezing water from the Interior and spilling them out in the hazed whorls of the sandy seaweed delta below the graveyard. Then I saw something.

Brotherhood heard my quiet laugh as he stood behind the Observation Lounge bar, drying a glass. He had on his dinner suit and bow-tie. The couple from number 6, sitting by the log fire, looked over in unison. It was so dark in the lounge by then I could only make out the man's eye sockets and was sure he was wearing a jet-black boilersuit below his neck.

Brotherhood sauntered to the wide panorama windows and lifted the binoculars from the peeling varnish of the sill to his face. In the middle distance the small, black aircraft-shape silently ascended again above the dark pines then swooped with a wobbling, dreamy, stilted manner, like a hallucination:

64

unnatural, not moving like a Real Thing, it came worrying down towards the walking figure until, this time, she chickened out and threw herself forward onto the sheer black of the cold ground. It was Chef Macbeth at the top of the airstrip, hiding at the fringes of the plantation, flying his radio-controlled model before dinners started. Brotherhood and I both laughed as the lithe figure stood up from the spoor of dark ground and moved towards us. The radio-controlled aircraft was over the spruces and gone.

Out on the Oyster Skerries the shipping lane auto-beacon began its eleven-second semaphore. Polaris, the North Star, flickered weakly above the waters of the Sound, sliding past, silently and ever-wide as some lugubrious Mississippi.

When the young woman's boots crunched on the buff gravel chips below, two things happened: weak, buttermilky moon reflected on the shoulder and arm of her black leather jacket and all the televisions suddenly switched back on as the signal came alive from up in the mountains where the aerial is. Brotherhood silenced them, his arm held out like a fascist salute.

As the girl moved round to the outside lamp by the corner of the building, I leaned back in the best armchair, away from my reflection on the black glass. I drained my whisky, letting the ice cubes rest against my lip, then I set the glass down.

'Well, well, *well*, real guest!' Brotherhood tossed the dish towel on the bar-top and moved down the spiral staircase to the reception area below.

I heard the front door open to admit the newcomer, then it opened a second time: Chef Macbeth with his aircraft under an arm, heading for the kitchens. I listened: no confrontation to help pass the evening.

I walked behind the bar and poured myself a large Linkwood fifteen-year-old, while there was still ice in my glass; I slopped in water from the decanter. Ignoring the stares from the number 6s I took up position on a bar-stool so we would be out of earshot when Brotherhood returned.

I heard the firedoors swing, then a few minutes later the different squeaking of them opening into the lobby. Brotherhood circled up the staircase, winked, swung behind the bar and carelessly tipped the neck of the Linkwood into his tumbler, gloshing a fair splurt over the edges which he ignored as he bit down the raw whisky, leaned over past the single beer pump, 'Fucking gorgeous, she could shove my toothbrush up her arse as far as it would go and I'd brush after breakfast and last thing at night. About twenty-four or five, seems to have come a long way over rough country. Where on earth's she wandered from to this place?' He paused then, concentrating; whispered, 'The wet lower material of her trousers was dappled with the burned golds of dead bracken. The arm of her leather jacket was streaked with mud and she was out of breath; she had a kitbag, held in a weird way . . .'

'What room did you put her in?'

'As I was SAYING,' (the number 6s gaped over), 'She held it out in front of her . . .'

'Maybe the straps bust?'

'So she had to look over it, the top of the kit-bag, and with her hair pinned up like that she seems even taller; she put down the kit-bag carefully, she said, "Do you have any vacancies?" I paused, surveyed her, then made a right show

66

of removing the register and flicking through it,' Brother-hood grabbed the bar menu and acted out the mocking turning of pages. He paused at desserts, looked at me from behind the menu. He stared at the sleeve of the cheap, functional outdoor jacket I bought in that Chandlers on the jetty at Ferry Slipway, one of two identical, even the same colour, *the cleanness, the purity of first days, my chunky new clothes, the incredible spirit of hotel rooms — monastic, assaulted daily by Chef Macbeth's fateful cauliflower and perpetual potatoes.*

Brotherhood said, 'I deliberately stared at the mud on her jacket sleeve in the hope it would unnerve her, but . . . made of sterner stuff this one.' He snapped the menu shut. "How many would the room be *for*?" "One," she said. "And for how many *nights*?" "I don't know. Three?" the little soul said.'

'Three! What one have you put her in?'

'"We. Are all. Fuuuullll. Up!"' Brotherhood leaned his chin on the bar-top then straightened up to full height. 'She just stared at me. Fantastic, cause she knew I was lying and she would huff to go walking back out into that night; then, perfect timing, Chef Macbeth appeared, walking in back-wards wearing that silly flying helmet, the big plane tipped up and held under his arm. Macbeth stared right over her shoulder at me, then laughed.' Brotherhood lowered his voice, 'she did not *even* turn round to look at Macbeth, just giving me the vicious eye on this room item. Single-mindedness. That's my kind of lass.' (The word said in that false way of those who have lost the accent and try to reclaim it.) Brotherhood smiled, 'So there's Chef Macbeth laughing out loud at the girl's shoulders. He's an illiterate runt but then you just had to hand it to him – give him his due. Anyway he cleared off to the kitchen with his toy aeroplane. I leaned to her a bit, breathing in gentle through my nose but I couldn't get any smell, no BO, no perfumes, nothing. I said, "I could give you a double room," sort of leered it. "That would be *good*," she came back with, completely deadpan, trying to make it as insincere as she possibly could.'

'You put her in 15.'

' "Sign here," I said to her.' Brotherhood took a card for registration from the pocket of his dinner jacket then slid it across the bar-top to me. I almost touched it with my fingers but held back and deliberately didn't glance down at what I knew was there: the fat, girly bubbles of writing on a card identical to the one Brotherhood had mockingly made me fill out on my day of arrival. Brotherhood stared at my face, hoping to catch my eyes trembling downwards: relishing the possibility of seeing me seek salvation in the pursuit of some pretty girl with healthy little stools who'd come rambling out of nowhere.

'Don't you think it's a lovely name?' Brotherhood taunted.

I looked down and the edges of my mouth curled as eyes rested, not on the name but the numeral 15 in Brotherhood's writing. I looked back up; the usual blankness, hiding the hope I'd given up, without memory of when, was all my face showed.

'I led her up the corridor.'

'Were you looking at her?' I was feigning interest, trying to play our game, staking a claim in Brotherhood's universe the way I'd been able to a month earlier when I began my investigation.

He replied, instantly, 'No. Obviously I was walking in front, striding into the darkness of the corridor before the sections lit up. When we got outside the room I was especially nasty because I stood talking without opening the door or handing her the keys that I'd kept, clutched in my hand all the time.'

'What were you saying?'

'The usual cack . . . "Perfectly respectable, my lovebirds, we fly them in; expecting a plane right now, explains the togs; I mean we're very informal here, up in our rather lovely lounge," now, mark my words and report back Sam Spade, give some credit to me cause I said . . . Ooops, shush.'

The male honeymooner from number 6 had stood and was crossing the dark lounge towards us, wearily swaying between the armchairs and circular tables.

'Yessss . . . sir.' Brotherhood showed his teeth.

'Is it okay to order food now?'

I didn't grace the guy with the curiosity of turning to even glance at his brand-new-wife's cream-stockinged legs, the lycra reflecting orange flames from the log fire. I knew everything; all was pre-ordained. On tonight's stroll, arm in arm around the concrete slabs forming two figure 8s in the pine plantation, the backs of those stockings would be splattered from the calves to the back of the knees with precise little dots of wet mud – even although it is a frosty night the slabs are laid so badly, mud is squeezed out from beneath as a foot is placed on each – those dots of mud will dry in the darkness, as each stocking lays concertina'd all night beside the bed in number 6.

'Here,' Brotherhood sliced the menu at him, 'The soup's broth. No . . . it's leek.'

The honeymooner crossed through the shadows to the safety of fireside brightness beside his young wife. They hunched over the menu.

There was no need to ask, I knew he would continue.

Brotherhood lowered his voice, 'I said, "Yes, very informal up in the lounge, big blazing log fire," I said to her, "Not *totally* informal though," that made her perk up a tad, "I mean we have exclusively married couples up there so nothing too provocative."'

I barked out a glut of laughter, genuinely in admiration of Brotherhood, I put both my palms flat on the bar-top, 'You're a genius, Brotherhood, that's just first-class, it really, really *is*!'

'Wait, wait,' he rocked back on his heels, 'What she said was, glaring at the keys I was fiddling with in my palm, "That's awful interesting, Mister," she used the word "Mister" the way a child would, "I don't have many clothes with me, they went down with that stinking little ferry that almost killed me, but rest assured if I had anything, it'd be so short, *soooo short* it'd be halfway up my butt. Don't *ever* tell me or any other girl how to dress – and can I have my keys?"'

'She walked into that one; let me guess when you're driving up to Far Places in the limo next?'

'Ummm, tomorrow?!'

We both laughed out loud. I said, 'Past the Wee Freeze . . .'

'Past The Best Little Hairhouse in Town . . .

70

'Into Horan's Fashions.'

'What size is she?' Brotherhood shrugged.

'Ten, the women I fall in love with are always size-ten tops.'

Brotherhood asked, 'Your wife?'

'That was before I left her, she'll've lost a lot of weight since I walked out.' I smiled defiantly, the pain only half cranked up through the whisky spookers. 'What's she say next?'

'Oh, come on, I think I'd a fine tactical opening created, it was all over to her. I sneered, held out the keys so they dangled down and she had to pick them rather than grab, "Make yourself at home . . ."'

'Wait, wait . . . you hadn't handed her the kitbag . . . ?'

'Steady on, Sam Spade, you don't think I'm carrying some women's libber's grenade launcher; she had it all the time – not looking as if she was letting go either – so I say, "Make yourself at home, I'll be seeing you up in the lounge later; we're serving dinner in ten minutes."'

I said, 'Wow, so she was Florence Nightingale on our latest Titanic.'

'Of course, aye, but let me finish my tac–au–tac; she asks, "Is the telly back on yet?" "Yes it is, it's just come on the minute you arrived, you brought a flooding of eternal bullshit with you."'

I smirked and flicked at my empty glass.

'By now she'd got the key in, opened the door and leaned, fumbled around to find the light switch, forced it on with her palm and seen there's no TV. She looks at me with real hatred, dead sexy. "I had the TV in this room taken up to my father; he's very ill in bed you know." "Can't I have a room with telly . . . ?" Telly, that's what she calls it. "No you cannot have a fucking tell–eh," I say, and feel like shoving her in the door but I said, "There are two in the lounge." "I'm *no* going up there" . . . *No* like that, "Oh yes you will be," I say, "The radiator doesn't work in this room," and I lean in and slam the door behind her.'

I was holding my chin down onto my chest with laughter, 'She'll be checking out at dawn, man!'

Brotherhood gave an inward look that startled me. 'I don't think so!'

I held up my glass and wiggled it, 'Charge this to room 15.'

We both laughed and Brotherhood replied, 'I will, you know I will!' he took the tumbler from my fingers and turned his back on me, I could see his hands pour out a large slap of sherry-cask whisky, not bothering with the measure; he stooped, removed the ice-tray, dropped three cubes into a glass towel, folded the fabric twice and with a serrated mallet suddenly and sharply pulverised the ice. The honeymooners from 6 actually stopped their hushed conversation. I smiled at the back of Brotherhood's dinner jacket, *I'll permit myself a foolish and private instant of an old croaking that I guess must be affection for this guy, dangerous and capable and at least a worthy enemy, out here on the edge of the world.*

Brotherhood sprinkled the ice splinters into the tumber, thudded it onto the bar then treated me by pouring the very cold water from the decanter himself; crushed ice tinkled up to the lip of the glass and he crossed through the shadows of the Observation Lounge to take the honeymooner's order.

A few of the honeymoon couples drifted up for feeding time, seething as usual, unhappy to be stuck for a fortnight with couples so identical to themselves; couples who, even with their talk of holidays, prudently hinted-at salaries, company cars and wedding days, were ultimately unable to differentiate themselves from each other. It was only slavish conformity to their desperate bid for happiness in wedlock that limited the infidelities and orgies that Brotherhood tried to orchestrate for his amusement.

I pushed my plate away, as usual never eating dessert. I'd had the scampi, assuming it would be safest; all Macbeth had to do was drop it in the deep frier. My fingers smelled of lemon when I lifted the last of the cheap cigars to my mouth.

'Plane in fifteen minutes; I just talked to him on the radio, low pressure coming in so he's straight out.' Brotherhood walked away from my table and began putting on his cashmere overcoat. I stood and tossed the paper napkin onto the plate.

Mrs Heapie had loaded two bottles of bad bubbly into an ice-box with four tall-stemmed glasses. I crossed to the bar. Chef Macbeth had on that silly flying hat (I suspected he kept it on while cooking).

We trooped down the spiral staircase and Brotherhood moved behind the reception desk to arrange the polaroid camera he trained on his latest victims.

'Got that drop-dead-gorgeous thing a beauty, eh?' Macbeth spluttered away.

I smiled.

'Stuka dive bomber, Nyeemmmm!'

*

'Shut up. Come on,' said Brotherhood and we stepped out the front door through the ridiculous fake Mexican portico. Outside in the dark we moved towards the staff caravans. Brotherhood looked directly up into the sky. There was low cloud but the ceiling was still acceptable.

'Just going to put my heater on,' Macbeth crossed over to his caravan. I shook my head but only under Brotherhood's eye. He corrected me with that look and strode off to the lean-to where the limo he'd bought off a yank at the old tracking station barely fitted. I tossed away the cheap cigar butt.

Chef Macbeth: his lithe shanks, the icy-blue arm tattoos, the police record left behind in two cities, the son he never saw – I knew it all without having to prise it from him over cans of cheap beer back in his caravan. This man fiddling away at his remote-control aircraft, the heart-breaking teariness in his eyes as he worked – his banal dumbness as he stood, stupefied, holding the control box with its outrageously long aerial, circling the aircraft round him. To come near to what Brotherhood had reduced this man to! Maybe that was why Macbeth carried the flick-knife I'd glimpsed in the single dirty navy-blue dress jacket he wore when they would watch Saturday comedy programmes; laughing towards the prettiest wives – the closest to intimacy he could get – jokes they didn't share but clutched to as a means of unity. By standing close to him (never laughing) I could peep down into the knife pocket. I could imagine Macbeth in stabbing mode – a whippity expression so you'd be more inclined to sneer and spit in his face rather than drop when he stuck you.

Brotherhood had Macbeth in complete control, refusing him any of the cars for the Saturday-night disco at The Outer Rim, baiting him with the possibility of another winter's employment, the reward of a hotel bedroom out of the caravan – earwig invasions in the rainy season, ants and mice in the heatwave.

Brotherhood had dumped the ice-box in the limo, crossed and unlocked the garage doors, 'You take the Volvo.'

I started it up, revving high and sliding the heater control to the red though only cold blew out. Chef Macbeth appeared in the Volvo headlights, slouching towards the wee van. I watched the tail-lights of the limo bump across the deep, circular tyre-ruts of the turning place. I revved up and followed, moving the gearstick into second. I braked as Chef Macbeth in the van came right up behind, headlights creating dark shadows inside the car with me.

In my full beams, Brotherhood parked, stepped out the limo with his open coat swinging. He marched the gate open and crossed in front of his headlights. Even when it was open I could read the angled sign . . .

AIRFIELD
NO ADMITTANCE
ACCESS TO
SHORE ON
LEFT

The limo accelerated ahead fast. I drove through the gateway; Macbeth peeled off to my left, his headlights swinging across the grass of the strip showing the life-belt on the jetty, momentarily lighting up a cold-looking birch sapling on the shoreline which I noticed had a piece of seaweed hung from one twig.

I followed the patches of limo headlights hovering across the grass towards the southern threshold. I accelerated up into fourth along the edge of the runway . . . a month since we had used the car headlights for a night-landing: there were no tracks on the grass. I hunched toward the windscreen, squinting, careful not to stray on to even the edges of the grass strip. At the threshold the limo veered over the far side and I angled the full beams ahead, out towards the river delta beyond the whin bushes. I pulled up the handbrake and, leaving the engine running, walked over to the limo with my hands in my pockets.

Brotherhood seemed startled when I appeared in the dark, just standing there. He jumped, leaned over and unlocked the passenger door.

'Jesus you nearly made me crap myself.'

'You must have a guilty conscience, or is it all the ghosts parading round this end of the runway that worry you?'

'Your ghosts,' he said. 'How is,' and he paused to curl up his lip, '*Work* going?' he kept staring out of the windscreen.

Cautiously, I said, 'I don't have the propeller from Alpha Whisky; I need a diver to go down and find it if it's at the end of the runway here. There are prop marks on one of the Hotel Charlie wings, I can calculate impact speeds by the distances between the gashes. I can tell all sorts by the prop, the exact angles of impact, pitch, engine conditions . . .'

'Quite the forensic scientist aren't you? When you're

chomping away on the bint from 15 I bet you can tell the blood type of the last man who squirted up there.'

I smiled, 'The answers are always there, in the wreckage; the answers are *always* in the wreckage, Brotherhood.'

For some reason, and I remember this clearly, Brotherhood murmured, 'Maybe it was a ghost last squirted up there.' Then he asked, 'Do you think, even if you got out the wreckage, you could swim that distance on a winter night in pitch darkness then climb up a hillside. . . ?'

'That's what happened. A night circuit and they crash into each other . . . right, it's their own fault for trying anything so crazy, but at the same time, as a professional, I've got to know exactly what happened. I know those planes were going in the same direction when they came in. Why did Alpha Whisky fly into Hotel Charlie?'

'And who gives a shit about happenings ten years' time ago; it won't bring the fellows back.'

'It doesn't matter, you dignify those horrible seconds of terror when you have it clear what happened. Like at Mount Osutaka when I was with the Boeing guys, we had five hundred and twenty dead up there and we were in in five hours. The rear bulkhead had collapsed and the Captain, I listened to that guy's voice, though he was talking Japanese, I was listening to the background noises on the cockpit voice recorder, as he was fighting for control; thirty minutes he kept that plane in the air, steering with his engines and what was left of the control surfaces. When he couldn't get it over Mount Osutaka there were no survivors. I was there, Brotherhood: broken pines, ravines, wrenched aluminium,

Dunlop tyres flopped skyward. And the bodies. Everywhere. Fatalities everywhere on the crash site and something I'd never seen before, everywhere, little notelets of paper, I bent to pick some up: on every one the little bamboo houses of Japanese writing, fluttering through all that shattered wood and burst suitcases and twisted limbs: goodbye notes. For thirty minutes they'd been in terror; what God lets you suffer thirty minutes just to die? Yet among that numbness they found time to pen words of farewell to the ones they loved. Even in extended death all we bother to do is confirm our love and say goodbye; what poems could equal those little notes?'

'Have you *quite* finished? There's nothing more revolting than hearing death sentimentalised. If the shitbang had gone up in flames those notes would have twirled heavenwards as ash. And your masterpiece? Incomplete.' Brotherhood looked at me and shook his head.

I said, 'I need to gather evidence. Aircrash Investigation frees you from causality: we're time travellers, obsessed with only a few seconds, minutes at most, of the past. All else becomes secondary and we live those moments again and again, until we've become part of the thing we investigate, we feel we effected that packet of time we weren't present for . . .'

Brotherhood put his head back and chuckled. 'I hand it to you; you're really something else.'

'Know anyone who'll raise the propeller if he can find it?' I smiled.

'I do actually, I mean if that'll really keep you happy and I think it might. There's a man they call The Argonaut. He doesn't come cheap,' Brotherhood raised an eyebrow.

'That girl must've swum ashore in the darkness with the Grainger child too.' I smiled over at him.

'Maybe we should dump her in the drink and see how she gets onto our island?'

'Maybe?' I said and Brotherhood seemed to perk up at the idea, then he nodded through the windscreen. I opened the passenger door and walked across to the Volvo in the cold air.

The landing light seemed to hang still in the air above the Sound. Fear was all I felt, the fear that had stuck with me through all I had done and said, through the women, the breaking hearts and empty achievements – the illness waiting inside of me. Then it was the fear of becoming part of Brotherhood's plans and the first suspicions that he planned to replace me with her, the newcomer in 15.

The moment she appeared on that skyline she was a threat to me and my cause; he only has three nights.

I ducked into the car and saw the droney pulse of the limo lights being dipped on and off. I began to flash my lights to the pilot. I turned round and saw the headlights of the van at the top of the runway, the blood-red caps fitted over both lamps marking where Macbeth had parked. The aircraft came over the so-called bay, where the sunken wreckage of Alpha Whisky lay in ninety feet of water seven hundred yards from the runway's end – apart from the wings that, in the impact, had been catapulted forward onto the machair by the plantation where the wreckage of Hotel Charlie had come down; all of it scavenged by local farms, initially for its macabre value, then finally incorporated into the walls of sheds and outhouses.

I saw the underwings of the nightflight (a Cessna 172) loom a hundred feet above then back over the Sound. As I always did with any night circuit of the field, I closely watched, winding down the window and trying to imagine it was that mythical night when two men died ten years before; the night that had come to spread out and fill my whole life with the events of those few minutes in the darkness.

I watched the landing lights lazily cross the Oyster Skerries beacon then the underwing revealed itself as he banked down-leg-final. His approach was a little high and hot: the limo swung round in a wide arc, its dipped headlights lighting up the interior of the Volvo. The limo accelerated up the runway after the lights of the aircraft which had touched down.

I motored up the side of the runway, mildly respectful of aviation regulations. When I came adjacent to the aircraft at the apron its propeller had stopped. I slowed to witness the usual farce: Brotherhood forcing glasses of bubbly on the two new couples (the men still in kilts). Chef Macbeth was loading suitcases into the back of the limo, 'The Love Mobile' Brotherhood would be calling it.

I revved in first gear through the gateway and reverse-parked the Volvo in the garage. I turned off the engine and tossed the keys in the glove compartment.

The vehicle ticked and tinkled secretly. I breathed out then stepped from the Volvo. The engine of the aircraft started up and I stood, hidden in the shadows, then strolled down to the gate with my hands in my pockets.

Brotherhood had taken the limo to the far end of the runway so the pilot had a clear perspective of where the grass strip ended. The aircraft throttled up and moved forward, its slipstream flattening out the longer grass behind it, so the sickly, pale blades seemed to create a faint phosphorescence in the plane's wake.

The aircraft bumped and swung out onto the airstrip, taxied way up to the threshold where it turned, pointing back down; it sat still, revved up to check engines and started the run.

My eyes focused and the nose seemed to lift, then it was off the ground. It passed about seventy feet up. The limo, with its lights dipped, came speeding down from the other threshold followed by the two blood-red eyes of the van. Brotherhood would be inside the limo, one of the new brides squealing as he drove straight for the newly risen aircraft.

The landing lights continued the climb-out over the Oyster Skerries. I turned and walked across the turning area towards the front door; illuminated by the bright limo lights, my shadow was sharp and clear then it swivelled and shrank on the mossy gravel. The tyres grushed past me and the white limo moved on to pull up outside the front door; then the sick, blood-red light from Chef Macbeth's wee van flooded the area, the colour seeming to run down the sides of the dirty-white staff caravans.

I stood still in the darkness, pretending to wait for Chef Macbeth. There was laughter as the limo door swung open, the young couples stepped out, the women holding a glass each, the men with both glasses and the bubbly bottles; they moved inside the foyer.

81

Beyond the caravan's calor-gas canisters I became aware of a feral movement out where the extension of rooms ending in 23 lay: arm in arm, circling among the pine plantation, were at least two honeymoon couples, strolling before using the sliding patio doors to their rooms. I had a speeding impulse to exterminate their composure in some way but since I heard Macbeth kill the engine on the van and the chassis judder to stillness, I stepped quickly forward, almost shivering at the thought of being invited into his caravan.

I passed the open boot and walked in the front door. Brotherhood was signing off with the pilot on the radio, the new couples were halfway up the spiral staircase; I scrutinised the wives' legs as they carefully circled. Brotherhood gave me a corrosive glance which meant, Get the luggage, while he quickly filled out the details of the aircraft's arrival and departure in the Airfield Log Book. He removed his cashmere overcoat and tossed it on the chair then selected four registration cards. Without a word I moved through the fire doors and marched up the long darkness of the corridor towards my room. The economy sensors detected my presence and the roof fluorescents came on, illuminating each section then switching off behind me so that – to Brother-hood, standing at the fire doors in the foyer, watching my departure, realising a battle had begun – I would appear to recede into infinite rectangles of clean, blue-tinged light.

I passed 15 without a side glance, put my key in 16 (the room the decayed pilot of Alpha Whisky had used); opened the door, clicked on the light and as I stepped inside, the corridor returned to pitch darkness. The door closed behind me and I crossed to the portable CD player, wound the Fourth Piano Concerto cassette to the Andante Con Moto to see if I could bleed a little more mystery from the pompous rubbish: all the rest of it sounded like fox-hunting music. I stooped to put on the telly and rewind the summer footage using the remote. I put the bedroom light off, lay on the bed and pressed PLAY.

The pale grey light from the images pattered around the room.

The camera had been switched on at the surface. Water flowed from the lens: the image was a man on the deck of a small boat passing a diving torch towards the camera, it was our very own toiler of the deep, Shan on board the hotel summer ferry *The Charon*.

The camera turned, not intentionally, showing low mist on the summer-lush slopes of 96-Metre Hill; I could pick out the very larch beside which the girl had materialised earlier in the day.

The camera submerged into the waters of the so-called bay at the end of the runway; blue silty water degenerating into a grey gloom. Bubbles and silt fluttered and stirred in front of the lens, silver against the submarine thickening and thinning of the light below. I took the remote and FF the descent until the Sound-bottom loomed up; moved over the heavily laden silt banks of the seabed . . . demersal fish lurked and darted everywhere.

I pressed PAUSE and rewound the portable CD to the start of the Andante then lay down again with the remote . . . PLAY . . . ahead, something loomed . . . slowly emerging from the grey-blue world came the upright dimensions of intelligent creation: the fin of the aircraft; sitting upright, the long wingless fuselage. *Looking as all human creations sunk in water look . . . eerie, dreamlike and forlorn*. Swishing the torchlight through the grey water, barnacles and encrustations adhered down the aluminium fuselage like a rash.

The camera moved along the wingless aircraft to the wider cabin, to the window on the side door. The view angled round as a hand came into frame; tried to pull open the door but it took three rapid, hard jerks before sheets of muck fell away and through a cloud of silt the door swung open. The diver jammed in the torch with its yellowing light. Everything went out of focus then came back in on a large horned lobster moving around inside the cockpit. *All the windshield is out. The fuel plunger is out but that could have happened on impact. The radio and part of the control panel appear to be out but it's fallen in, behind the panel . . . those once-ordered instruments . . . it's the image of everything that's hostile to us.*

The camera backed out, then it must have been switched off. It cut to the blunted front of the aircraft: engine torn, laying metres away, but the propeller missing. I pressed REW ◁. overshot; FF ▷, PLAY □: the engine mounting came up close and, while in focus, PAUSE □□: the prop bolt seemed to have been sheared.

Thoughts: 1. Prop disintegrated on impact, wreckage not recoverable.
2. Prop damaged in the water.
3. Though impractical in outhouse construction, prop scavanged from machair crash site by unknown party.

There was another cut in the footage then it came on again. A torch had been placed inside the cockpit. The camera started high on the tailplane and I could distinguish the registration marking ending A W beneath the black fuzz of sea-growth. The shot moved along the side of the plane, an off-camera arm opened the cockpit door with the golden torch lighting it from within. *Very* artistic.

The film cut to a shot of the forward landing wheel, torn off, slivers of silt tracers attached to the tyre leaned side to side in the current, the fuselage in the distance and, above all this, the cathedral gloom of light rays down to that tomb world of inner space.

He must have got out through the bust windshield . . .

A loud hammering began on my door making me leap forwards then freeze. I hurled my legs down on the carpet, stood and switched off the Rondo Vivace. I was furious with myself because as I stepped towards the door I was terrified. *He has reduced me to this.* I paused, turned and put the video on PAUSE □□. The door thundered again. I stepped to it and tugged.

'Play it loud though I'm trying to sleep but – deal – I get to choose the music,' she held out a reflective disc that caught and threw about the fluorescent strip on the corridor ceiling above her. I realised it was a CD. She was wearing a big man's shirt and her legs were bare. She'd washed her hair and its shape had changed. I'd only seen her before in the darkness, at a distance. Now a longing I thought I'd conquered years before slapped into me, as if it were a sheet blown on a vast beach.

'It's Beethoven. I loathe it but it's the only cassette in the place apart from the one Brotherhood plays up in the lounge; know what that's called?'

She looked at me. Later she would claim her eyes were dark blue but that night she knocked on my door my notes indicate they were darkest black (Brotherhood would always scoff, insist they were dark green).

I said, 'The Emotion Collection'. I'm not sure if the CD works; there aren't any CDs, unless he's some hidden upstairs with all his Bob Dylan records,' I didn't know whether to retreat back into the room and try the CD; I was afraid she would leave. She shifted herself to look beyond me.

'Hey, you've a video.'

'He gave me it for my work.'

'What films've you got?'

'Ah, I don't have any.'

'What?!'

'None, I've no films.'

'What's that?'

'It's a sunken aircraft.'

'A sunk aircraft. You know how to get your kicks, Ludwig, you really do.'

'Do you want to watch it?' I shrugged, then was glad to find myself laughing.

'That's your job isn't it? You investigate why planes crash.'

'I'm a civil servant,' I shrugged, 'How do you know?'

She tapped her forefinger against the side of her nose. The fingernail had ruins of nail varnish on it. She sighed and said, 'No much else going on is there,' and stepped in the room.

She sat on the bed which wasn't made (I refused Mrs Heapie access to the room and the young woman was the first person to enter it) pressing down the end of the mattress.

I picked up the remote control and felt a bit foolish, as I rewound the footage, saw the camera scuttle surfacewards back up the anchor rope.

I let the tape run forwards. She watched without saying anything. I stared at the screen. When I stepped awkwardly in front of her to the CD machine she moved her head slightly to look past my leg. The CD spun wildly when I inserted and it began to play.

'Oh great,' she said and sang the chorus bit. 'Where is this plane? It's pretty amazing I guess.'

'It's here, at the end of the airstrip off from the ruined chapel. The guy that was in it died.'

'Aye?'

'Aye,' I said. 'He bashed into another plane when they were flying round the airfield at night when you shouldn't be doing that. There are no landing lights on this strip. They were both experienced pilots; should have known. They'd had dinner up in the Observation Lounge: some wine, glass of brandy, girlfriends to impress, so they dared each other. The aircraft in the lead, it came down on the field you crossed today, this one came down in the water. They never found the body, gave up the search then; weirdly, months later, they found the guy way up the hillside, you passed it as well, the spot they found his body.'

'Had he fallen out the sky there?'

'No, that would be impossible, he'd died of exposure. It

was winter weather like this when they crashed; somehow he got out the wreckage and swam ashore. He must've been terribly concussed or disorientated. He could have walked right here. This was his hotel room; he could have walked it in ten minutes, but he climbed right up the open hillside and must've died up there. He crossed three barbed-wire fences. He must have thought he was on the other side of the Sound or something, God knows. I've lain for ten years trying to work it out; it's tragic to get out of a mess like that,' I pointed to the screen, 'And die of the cold up a hill.'

She humped her shoulders, 'This was his room?' She looked round at me.

I nodded, 'Want to see a picture of him?'

'A picture of him; what, after he'd swum ashore and gone up there?'

'Yes.'

'You mean a photo of his rotted body?'

'I have the police photos if you're interested, you being bored and all.'

She shifted on the bed a little; then, in a new, clearer, challenging voice, 'Show me.'

I opened the drawer, took out the envelope, polished by hands, dropped it on the bed beside her. She slid them out and I was pleased to see the worst one was on the top, the shirt undone showing the dark drop inside, through the rib-cage. She slid it out and put it to the back then flipped through the others.

'Hoody crows,' I smiled.

She nodded then suddenly held up the skull-faced black

eyes and pointed to the man kneeling beside, hair longer: Brotherhood . . . She gave a grimace.

'Pilot lay there five months, some hill-walkers found him. Brotherhood was over on holiday before he came back to run this place.'

'Tell you what I think. Put the CD on again. My plane comes down in the night-darkness, aye?'

'Right.'

'I scramble out the plane and in the sheer pitch blacknesses I manage to swim ashore.'

'You're the expert.'

She folded up her very smooth forehead at me. 'News travels fast on this island.'

I hunched my shoulders.

'When I get ashore — and it's hard to know what way to swim in the dark towards shore unless you spot some kind of light, headlights on the road maybe — then, *why* did he cross the road?'

I smiled at her.

'Now, I've seen those flashing lights out on the rocks there and I'm sure he saw them too, if they'd been built ten year ago?'

'They had yes.'

'So he'd gumption enough to use them to swim in. He knew exact where he was. Now this is where it gets interesting. If you come ashore in that darkness, and I've done it; it crosses your mind you're back from the dead. Ever read *Pincher Martin*?'

'Yes.'

'You feel an excitement. I'd come ashore with some daft wee child. It'd crossed my mind if she wasn't with me I'd be free. Free to vanish. It's an incredible feeling. Your man had come back from the dead. His plane had crashed into another and fallen to the sea. When he got on the stones of the shore he wanted to use that power. That choice to be dead, to be ghost, escape off the island somehow, start a new life; so in first flush he takes wide strides up the hillsides . . .'

'Within twenty minutes of the planes crashing they started searching the hillsides with torches . . . !' I said, excitedly.

'Right, right, so he's hiding up there, still trying to make that decision to step over to the other side. To get vanished. He has family, people he's convinced himself he loved. He flies, so he has money, so he's a bastard, yes?'

'Well . . . not everyone . . .'

'You can fly a plane, eh? You must if you investigate . . .'

'Ah. I don't actually. I can't fly, I'm more on the engineering side. Brotherhood flies.'

'Point made. So this guy has house, car, wife, family, a lover, all the usual crap; playing little boys in aeroplanes. But up there he faces the first real decision of his life. Choose himself for the first time or . . . he can see the torches now, all he needs to do is walk down to the hotel. He's shivering now. It's bitter, bitter up there, he sees the light calling him back to the world but it's one of lies. Lies.'

I said, whisperedly, 'He chose himself but it was death.'

'Aye, so. How about a bit of telly?'

I leaned in with the remote but as I flicked from station to station each was a flurry of white dots.

The girl said, 'Oh, noo! Don't believe it, it's out again!'

'Aerial is always going in this weather.'

'Aye. Met the guys who fix it, a team of them were on the wee ferry that sunk, what a crew, chuck them in a barrel of tits and they'd come out sucking their thumbs.'

I said, 'Ah, that pilot, from the hillside where he rotted, that one's buried in the graveyard over by the river mouth.'

'Oh. Right. What's his name?'

'Carlton. William Carlton.'

'Right. Any chance of borrowing your ghetto-blaster there. My Walkman got cabbaged in my wee capsizing.'

'If you do me a favour in return,' I said, and I saw her head keep deliberately still but she'd seen the one-inch-open patio door where the crisp corner-curled net curtain was hanging back.

'What?'

'Stay here your three nights. Gawp at the circus and try to keep out of Brotherhood's schemes – whatever you get your kicks from – then get your schoolgirl's arse out of this place and never come back.'

She carried on staring at me then said, rapidly, 'And I thought you were a goody. Why *should* I?'

'You'd have a nicer time in other places.'

'Threat?'

'You know.'

She laughed but it wasn't convincing, 'You're really starting to interest me, Mr Civil Servant Man.'

'Don't take the piss, Kylie Minogue. You're out your league in Drome Hotel.'

She stood up and made for the door. 'Does our deal stand?'

'For three nights as loud as I want but your CD.'

'Three nights . . . to start with,' she said and definitely did not do any looking back.

I took off my clothes and climbed into bed. I let the CD music run on; it was some young-sounding band, moaning on with a real enthusiasm. These young pessimists; what a joke – all day long they lament the darkness of the universe then drink all night and at six a.m. you can bet they won't be shitting a peptic ulcer out their still-tight arseholes. They want everything – even the right to pessimism; they won't accept it's a pleasure reserved for those of us over thirty.

I pulled up the sheet round me, holding its edges as if another human being was in bed with me. I thought of the only dream I would have: cigars . . . Havanas . . . The Real Thing. I took pleasure in my drowsiness with that relish for the simplistic found in most doomed men.

Sunday the Fifteenth

From my notes of that day:

8 a.m. That drugged-out alcoholic's helicopter passed over the runway with a large grizzly bear dangling beneath in a netting.

Stool: colicky/green. Certainly no darkenings of blood from a – for instance – ruptured rectum.

In the afternoon I had to walk to that old bastard Gibbon's Acres to barter for the left cabin door of Hotel Charlie. There was no sign of the Newcomer around the hotel.

Smoke-like mist was tight down on the low slopes of 96-Metre Hill above me. Across the Sound the ragged, torn line of vapour ran along the mountain range. I tugged up the hood on the functional jacket then trotted down to the shore, legging up shingle until I had walked along as far as I could at the rocks. I stepped up onto the Big Road verge. Because of the hood, my view to the rear had been obscured for so long that when I finally turned around, with a shock, the view I thought so familiar to me seemed suddenly foreign, as if I were seeing it for the first time. As if my experiences pacing out the dimensions of every metre on the runway were simply rehearsal.

The mile of shoreline to the delta beyond the graveyard, the slow-moving tidal waters of the Sound, the hotel, its outbuildings, the boathouse where I was re-constructing the two doomed planes, the Celtic crosses of the ruined chapel among the pine plantation by the airfield: all these constituted my universe and my future. But my familiarity with those dimensions, every piece of earth covered by my own feet – that certainty was gone for a bewildering instant, then just as suddenly it leapt back to me and I recognised this land I saw. I frowned and walked on.

Mr and Mrs Heapie passed in their ancient Austin and I nodded grudgingly. Joe the Coal passed in his ex-Army Bedford and I waved.

The jacket was heavy with drizzle when I reached the long, puddled dirt track to Gibbon's farmhouse. Old Gibbon was working in the outhouse itself with a clown: the Knifegrinder. I walked to the side wall: the lower sections of the bizarre barn were constructed out of heavy railway sleepers, which in itself was unusual because there was never a railway on the island, save the miniature affair along at the military zoo. Cheap plywood had been nailed onto the sleepers and now warps and curls were prising gaps of light between the boards. Gibbon had been delighted to find an economical way to get a lick of something waterproof to douse the boards. He'd been too mean to buy paint: when the biscuit bakery at Far Places had gone bust, Gibbon had taken away gallons of raspberry food-colouring from the auction. To his amazement, the stuff was completely waterproof; the lower sections of the outhouse were soon crucially pink: raspberry pink. As a paint it proved sturdy enough but the outhouse's downfall came when Gibbon's cattle strayed from the fields into the yard and began licking the walls. Not only did they remove all the colouring up to five feet round the structure, the constant licking and pushing of the cattle wrecked sections of the walls and Gibbon had to fence off the outhouse to keep it from destruction.

I crossed the muddied yard. The upper sections of the building, where the cabin door to Hotel Charlie was incorporated, was a hodge-podge of corrugated iron, the side walls of a caravan, plastic greenhousing material, unidentifiable sheets of metal and see-through plastic and even an old island road sign, so a large side section of the wall read:

'Hullo,' I yelled. The door was on the far side of the outhouse so I'd called out before marching around to it.

The two men, who were hunched over Knifegrinder's motorbike which he used to turn the sharpening stone with some kind of belt mechanism, suddenly swung round together – which surprised me, since the noise of the bike inside the outhouse must have been quite bad. The Knifegrinder had a selection of douse-slashers and scythes laid out before him. Both men looked at each other then the Knifegrinder's arm went out and he killed the motorbike.

I found myself standing outside – exactly opposite where the Hotel Charlie door was fitted above the bank of sleepers and licked plywood; misshapen bits of metal rose up to the ceiling like a geodesic dome in a scrapyard.

Gibbon crossed to where I stood, effectively a non-invitation to the interior of the outhouse. Strangely, the door of Hotel Charlie separated us and Gibbon reached up and slid the actual perspex window of the door open.

'Aye-aye, how're you doing?'

'I've brought the compensation forms.' I unfolded one of the forms I'd reproduced on the photocopier behind the reception at The Drome. I handed it through the open window of the aircraft door.

Gibbon removed the broken spectacles from his boilersuit pocket and put them on. The Knifegrinder came striding up behind him and began tirading, 'It's legitimate salvage that, it's legal landfall, you'd best be getting a good price . . .'

'It's up to him to put an estimate,' I snapped.

'Well look here now, mmmm, last summer I lost a Suffolk,

lovely Suffolk offof the maggots; broke its horn, maggots get in there off the fly and ate out its brains. I'll claim back the price for that. One thousand six hundred.'

I had to smile. Gibbon strolled off, the compensation form stretched out in his big hands as he walked forwards to the sheets on the floor with the array of scythes and implements.

'How will we get it down?' I asked.

Gibbon looked up at the aircraft door in the patchwork of debris, 'Hell, man, give it a tug and it'll come away there.'

I took hold of the shiny door-handle and pulled: the wall area ballooned outwards. I put my palm against the section of road sign to the left and saw the bits of metal had been spot-welded and roughly rivetted, most of the holes round the rivets had rusted, with sorry, drooping stains trailing downwards.

'One thousand six hundred!' The Knifegrinder was looking between me and Gibbon, 'Your department'll pay that? Man I'll track down your bits of planes.' He leapt up at the window on the aircraft door, hanging on with his fingers: the entire wall wobbled inwards then out on his weight, the Knifegrinder drooled at me.

I whispered, 'Ever hear of a propeller? I wonder how much the Department would pay for that?'

'Propeller? Propeller! Yess, I can find you one . . .'

'Yeah, but it's gotta be the *right* propeller.'

Gibbon was calling, 'Hi, let go of that door or you're going to be bringing down the whole contraption . . .'

'Propeller . . . thousands . . .' The Knifegrinder's eyes rolled back and he held his face up to the ceiling, the door ripped out and his weight on the window edge suddenly forced it down so he stumbled forwards and bounced off the railway sleepers; I saw him bent over, cavorting sideways: the whole wall creaked then juddered. I grabbed the door at the hinge where it had folded with the Knifegrinder's weight, hoisted it up and stepped back from the structure as more bits began to fall – what seemed to be the aluminium hull of a flat-bottomed boat, another road sign, a bedboard: all came a-tumbling down.

I swayed away from the crashing as sections of the ceiling collapsed. I held the left cabin door of Hotel Charlie awkwardly under my arm as I hurried up the pot-holed driveway. I passed it across a fence, clambered over myself, then lifted the door and began a short cut over the foothills to skirt the back of 96-Metre Hill, avoiding the camp of the Devil's Advocate.

I found the door painful to carry uphill. Soon I opened the window and placed my head through it, holding the door up with both hands, around me like a collar; the sun blustered through the vapours, burning like a necklace of fire around my head on the raw aluminium where the white and blue paintwork was scratched away or had lifted off.

I moved up and down the slopes, wary of the grass, reduced to slime in the lee of some hills by the weeks of rain.

Under the brief sun I descended into the silver clouds of a shower below the camp of the Devil's Advocate; I knew the shivers of sunlight still racing across the slope flanks would be falling on the bare aluminium of the door, crashing flashes over to the man at his camp as I tried to steady my way down the lands. I paused at one point both to lift my face to the larch where Carlton was found and to indicate a challenge to the Devil's Advocate to come down to the hotel and battle on my terms.

I took the cockpit door of Hotel Charlie to the boathouse. Under the single bare bulb I walked over the rounded tiles of the floor, leaned the door against the bent fuselage of the aircraft; the shattered wings were supported on beer crates from the hotel, to bring them flush with the top of the cabin where the pilot was killed, his rib-cage flattened by massive deceleration injuries and the impact of the engine being driven through the instrument panel, severing both his feet. I had seen the photos of that corpse too, with the massive contusions to the facial area.

The fuselage was too distorted to be able to fit the door in roughly its original position. I stood awhile in the space I'd kept clear for the wreckage of Alpha Whisky, the black tiles swept by myself after Brotherhood granted me the boat-house. Each round, black tile beneath my boots was an inverted champagne bottle, plunged into concrete by Brother-hood himself in the 1970s, before he wearied with boating.

I walked back to my room to wash and change. I could hear nothing from the bathroom of 15 as I lifted water to my own face and thought of Carlton hitting the Sound in darkness and the fear he must have felt.

I liked to arrive early for dinners to display my connections with our leading family. I spun up the spiral stairs two at a time: Brotherhood, Macbeth (in chef whites!) and Mrs Heapie were all there and turned to look at me. As I strolled towards them a lump rose in my throat, like when I watch the saddest movies; I looked at the spotlights shining down on the bar, the chairs and table stretching off into the darkness then coming against the burnished ambience of the brass frieze, the log fire fumbling a few shadows up the brass to the point it met the pine-panelled ceiling. The frieze was of a sinking Armada ship, its masts at a stricken angle. *It's the only home I have now.*

'It's Mad Max,' called Brotherhood and the others smirked. Heapie was on her third courtesy coffee, I would have guessed, and her third cigarette; one dimpled elbow hung by her side.

'Yon lassie in 15; ah could't get in all day for her sleeping! I'm no putting up with it; can make her own bed,' Heapie mumbled off into an inhalation, then perked up looking out into the near-dark, 'Oh look, here comes Shan. Who'll be this coming over?'

'Usual?' said Brotherhood, not smiling.

I nodded and Brotherhood poured a small Linkwood then dropped a single, half-melted ice-cube in. He placed it in front of me and just for a second I thought he was going to ask me for the money.

'I'll charge that to 16,' he stated.

Mrs Heapie had crossed to the panorama window and watched the lights of *The Charon* coast into the jetty and secure. Two figures wearing anoraks scaled the ladder up onto the pier. I yawned. The young walkers didn't cross the airfield, distinguishing them as non-locals. I heard Mrs Heapie exhaling over by the broad glass.

'Aye, that's Shan way back over again!' she announced. As if obeying her, the launch cast off and moved astern.

Unable to endure any more of Heapie's Commentary On Everything, I stood, stretched and walked to the farthest table-for-one where I sat down. Brotherhood gave me a cruel smile. I smiled back, shook my head. *You are standing there twisting a paper napkin between your fingers and you're about to put on The Emotion Collection for the arrival of the first couples, but I know you're just waiting for her to appear: I hope she stands up to you, hope she is worthy, her only defence might be her virtue. If she has any.*

Couples began to converge on the Observation Lounge. Mrs Heapie was serving in her tartan skirt, Brotherhood worked behind the bar and transferred the meals from the kitchen lift.

Mrs Heapie tried to put me down by stopping at my table before bringing me cutlery. I countered her: 'Bring me a Remy Martin, the deluxe, with crushed ice and mineral water.'

'What are you eating?' she snapped.

'I haven't decided . . . Mrs Heapie.'

Defeated she walked away. I sighed. *I feel jubilant, close to a victory, like when I was twenty-five.*

Brotherhood crossed over with my drink, 'Good evening.'

'How the devil are you!' slapping him just above his buttocks. He was lost for a reply, the idiot, so I said, 'Let's set sail on the sea of dreams.'

'Yes let's,' he nodded.

I winked at him and, pretending nonchalance, Brother-hood strode off.

I took healthy swallows of the cognac, even recognised one of the couples who had arrived the previous night. From Heapie's monologues I knew they were in either room 12 or 11.

Heapie returned, 'Made up your mind, then?'

'I'll have the soup, whatever it is.'

'It's lobster bisque,' she leaned over, horribly near, her huge breasts almost touching the tablecloth; she whispered, 'Canned.'

'Forget the soup,' I thought of the monster in the cockpit of the plane on the seabed. 'What else is there?'

She leaned back as if about to spit, hugely, on me.

'Melon. Prawn.'

'Melon, I'll have that. What's for main course, I mean if you'd brought me a *fucking* menu!' I shouted. All the honeymoon couples looked over.

'Entrecote steak, vegetable pie. Fish.'

'Get me a steak, very well done, don't let Macbeth piss on it, and clear my plate when I've finished. I'm going to have a dessert.'

'You never have a sweet.'

'Aye, well I am tonight. I've got a sweet tooth, Mrs Heapie.'

The melon was foul; Macbeth must have had it in the fridge since it was dessert the previous week – it turned to a hardly-sweet mush the second it was dropped on the tongue. I picked at two pieces – ate the grape off the top – all the time staring at the railings of the spiral staircase. My attention dived over there each time a head appeared, though each materialised into the linked, dual heads of a couple arm in arm. *Oh for someone with a bit of independence.*

A few voices stopped talking and I looked up. More voices should have stopped. Her arms were bare and tanned, she was wearing black Levi's but she disarmed that long-tight-jeans look by the neat, battered boots she was wearing and she'd wrapped a baggy cardigan round her and fastened it at the waist. I glanced at Brotherhood and a selection of supposedly happy, newly-wed men, regretfully watch her crossing the floor.

I stood, took two steps towards her: all the couples' heads followed me but it was Brotherhood's face I was watching. She wore a necklace: a gold chain so thin and fragile at first I mistook it for a strand of hair that fell and tumbled.

'Join me in this poisoning experience,' I mumbled, head averted away from Brotherhood's gaze.

'Aye, all right then,' she shrugged.

She ordered (vegetable pie) and we ate in silence, sometimes a smile: me raising eyes to heaven when Mrs Heapie collected plates. Our complete silence infuriated the audience more than anything. I gobbled down the stringy, underdone steak, the powdered potatoes. I asked for bread and wiped my plate.

'Let's have a sweet,' I said.

'Why?'

'Because desserts are funny,' I said.

'I understand what you've got against them; you really want to eat them but you never ever do, eh? You think I can't fathom it out but I *can* fathom it out, normally you're just the old grump basically . . .'

I laughed. Heads turned.

'. . . No, let me finish, you think you're above such things whereas you're really a sport but you don't like saying the names of the things, 'cause you take life so seriously, which in a way shows how amazingly childish you are. If you had kids of your own you might not be so gloomy about just words on a menu. You don't, have you?'

'Nope,' I said.

Mrs Heapie crossed to our table and the girl said, 'Two Double Whammy Choc Dollops please.'

After the sweets she wanted tea. The Observation Lounge was emptying. Down in the pine plantation the crazed couples would be circling in their futile little ballet of desire.

Brotherhood had waited his moment and suffered. As the last of the couples left he crossed to where we sat.

'Everything all right?' he laughed at us.

'Aye, alright,' she said. I almost clenched my teeth. She was out her depth and too near the edge for Brotherhood.

'And your room?'

'Bracing.'

I smiled.

'I'll change your room the night after tomorrow, we have a couple leaving.'

'Oh, it's okay,' she looked at me, 'I'll be toddling on by then.'

I smiled directly at her but couldn't stop myself wondering if she would give me her address. *No. It's out the question; it's dangerous here.*

'Oh, such a shame, when you've made interesting friends.'

Correctly, she just smiled back at him and he put down the tray of tea things for her.

'Where on earth did you *come* from?' Brotherhood unashamedly asked. *He doesn't care. Years have passed and he no longer remembers how to compromise. Like me he's long wearied with that petty triumph as a girl's body resignedly slumps against you.*

'Just the Mainland and that.'

'Just the Mainland! You should be careful coming over the hills without proper walking gear. We've already had two deaths in this place and my Daddy, whose *telly* you wanted to steal, is about to croak upstairs; last thing we want is our mountain rescue cursing you and picking up your limp corpse from the hillsides – there's no telling what our helicopter pilot Nam would do to your corpse if he had it alone for a while. *So*! You're a local . . . you *sound* like a native. That cursed Port itself?'

'No tiene nada que ver contigo, abuelo,' she muttered.

'Woh! Gloria Estefan. So you're not quite the local and that would explain the suntan. You've been away?'

'But now – I'm back.'

'Yes, back, seeing the lovely sights that others pay so much to see, especially in *my* hotel, but *we*, on the other hand, can see for *nothing*, mmm?'

'Whatever you say,' she said. I almost jumped up and clapped. Brotherhood nodded, angry now, but a loving smile still on his face.

'Now, let's see,' Brotherhood gazed over at the black glass of the panorama window, 'What do we know about you? We know your name, though it's so ridiculous I must presume it's a lie, you must have a passport but you've never volunteered it. Tut tut. You're from the Mainland – tell that by accent – but you've been away a long time: by the sounds of it licking dago. We know you're back and we know you're here, but where are you going?'

'I'm going to my bedroom for a cup of tea,' she smiled and stood, carefully lifting the tea-tray up from the table.

'I mean, you're only staying with us three nights and you haven't stepped out to see our lovely pine plantation and heather beds, and you missed breakfast this morning and that's included in the price!'

'I don't eat breakfast,' she said flatly.

I was sitting, smiling softly at the spectacle. I could see Brotherhood was desperate for a weakness in her.

'You don't eat breakfast!' he was spluttering.

'Careful on the stairs,' I said. The girl turned and smiled at me.

'I will be. If you really want to know, Brotherhood,' she announced, 'My foster-mum is buried along the shore there, *right.*'

So that's why she took so long to cross the machair, she must have visited right then.

'Goodnight,' she called.

106

'Goodnight,' I replied, leaning round Brotherhood. Holding the tray before her she gently descended the stairs, her hair smoothly sinking down into the orange carpet and she was gone.

Brotherhood glared at me.

I shrugged, 'She popped in to say hello last night. I told her to clear off out of here.'

'You boned her?'

'No. She's not interested in the likes of me or you, she's bigger time than us,' I said.

Brotherhood walked back to the bar shaking his head. He poured himself a whisky, thumped down in the seat she'd been sitting in then took a long stare at me. 'You sad, sad man,' he stated.

I shrugged my shoulders then suddenly, amazed I hadn't realised before, I saw he was onto me.

'How long have you known?' I said.

'Since the first few days.'

'That long?'

'You interest me; you amuse me; and I can call Sgt McGilp whenever I want. What I'll have to do tomorrow, though, is give a wee seminar on you to your girlfriend there.'

'Don't be a bastard, she wouldn't heed my warning.'

'Oh, listen to you squeal,' he smiled.

It was stupid but time was running out for me and I so much wanted to wipe the smile from his face. 'Where do you keep it Brotherhood?'

His whole posture changed and his eyes widened out, 'My God, you're really amazing.'

I said, barely a whisper. 'I always wanted to know about that crash, about Carlton, I always had an interest. It was that led me here; you're just a fringe benefit.'

Brotherhood contemplated his tumbler, 'You haven't even the excuse of being drunk. Behave, Aircrash Investigator.'

He stood up and walked over to the log fire, pokered it down and rolled the wood to burn safely in the middle. 'Put out the lights,' he smiled and then added, 'You know, you think you've stepped over too many shocking sights, with honour grinning up at you, dismemberment, mutilation, fatalities: all part of your daily vocabulary. You've already walked through the apocalypse . . . but don't forget, that's all in your dreams – that's what you *want*. What kind of person are you? Men. All devils. What do you think chased Carlton up that dark hillside?' He walked down the staircase, sinking into the floor in the half-light; I turned and saw the lone beacon of the Oyster Skerries blink hopelessly.

I turned out the lights, made my way downstairs. I sashayed medium-joyously up the corridor, the night closing behind me.

Monday the Sixteenth

Another morning was spilling all over the island. I watched the summer footage, walked up the corridors to have a good breakfast, keep watch over the girl through the day then send her on her way the following morning.

Only two couples were in the Observation Lounge, both dressed for departure on an incoming aircraft. I glanced at the cloud base which was high enough above the drizzle through the panorama windows.

I imagined the breakfast Macbeth would place before me. The golden, burned fringes of the fried egg-white: bubbled like treacle toffee; the watery tea I would oversweeten.

Macbeth crossed towards me. I presumed he was about to say 'tea or coffee?' and I had aleady inhaled to make my reply (he in chef whites and checks, the bottom of his clean trousers flapping as he crossed the orange carpet). 'Heard the news? Drop-dead-gorgeous-bint's staying another week.'

I stood, the man in chef's clothes and the four youngsters in overcoats and wedding rings on the four fingers all looking at me.

'Where is she?' I said, not whispering.

'Went out. Twenty minutes ago, wouldn't have a coffee even. I asked!'

I zipped up my jacket as I walked away from him: outside, the drizzle seemed to stand in columns. I walked quickly past the garages and staff caravans. Up at the top of the pot-holed drive I turned left and walked along the Big Road verge; beyond the bridge I looked over to the melancholy blue plastic ribbons I had cordoned off the crash site of Hotel Charlie with: twisted and thrumming in the stiff breeze. I turned along the pathway, approaching the enclosures of the graveyard and the gable end of the ruined, pre-Reformation chapel. I spotted her at the far end of the machair across the graveyard. I was more than familiar with every gait: Brotherhood's, Macbeth's slouch, Mrs Heapie's ponderous progress down the drive on a Sunday or the distant and conjoined conferring of a circling honeymoon couple. Her walk was still young, energetic and heart-breakingly confident – boyish too. Her figure vanished behind the graveyard walls and I tried to cut her off at the gate by plunging into the boggy moor grass, puddles like chunks of dark glass among the reeds; I missed one, my foot sunk, I sighed and stepped backwards, wiping the sides of my boots on a grass tuft.

I walked down the Sound side of the graveyard, past the Celtic crosses that abutted above the wall and the hideous headstones supplanted with grievous angels that turned their lichen-covered shoulders to the waters of the so-called bay.

Stood up on the wall with one outstretched arm rested upon the head of an angel was the girl. She raised the other arm, gave a wave, jumped and vanished behind the stones.

I ran back to the gate and strode up the central path of the small graveyard. She was standing beyond Carlton's plot, in front of a headstone. Her hair wasn't covered in any way, it was so wet it had coagulated into thick dark cables and she'd pushed it away from her forehead.

'I thought there was a roof on it,' she smiled and nodded to the chapel ruin. The little digger machine used by the council for making new graves (and delivered there, as surreptitiously as possible, from the graveyard on the other side of the island, when Brotherhood's father worsened) was parked in the lee of the chapel, covered in tarpaulin. Before I could speak she veered over to the digger. She tugged at the plastic and said, 'We can use this,' kneeled and started undoing a toggle on the plastic. A flap came away, but by holding it over her head with both hands she could shelter under.

I said, 'Why are you staying on here, in this forsaken place, this bloody brothel and that ridiculous man; can you not use your perception to see the man's the Devil. *All* you need to do is take a bus or taxi out of here, cut your holiday short for God's sake?'

There was a low groaning sound, a splatter of movement up in the cloud and the red wings of a Piper Cherokee sliced out, over the bay towards us; as it passed, she pulled away the tarpaulin and, squinting into the rain, turned her face up to follow the aircraft that went straight in, clouding out a sheath of spray when it came over the threshold and touched down on the grass.

'You'd better get out of here. Take yourself over to The Outer Rim Hotel. They've got people your age there. And a disco.'

She smiled, 'But you can get a bus on the Saturday nights from the end of the drive, The Disco Bus; Chef Macbeth told me.'

'Don't listen to Chef Macbeth, don't listen to any of the people here!'

'Mmm,' she nodded. She removed something from her leathery jacket, handed it to me.

DEAR MR BROTHERHOOD,

FURTHER TO YOUR FAX THIS MORNING AND OUR TELE-PHONE CONVERSATION. I CAN FIND NO TRACE THAT HE WAS *EVER* AN EMPLOYEE OF THE AIR ACCIDENT INVESTIGATION BRANCH AND THE BRANCH WILL COVER *NO* EXPENSES WITH REGARD TO HIS ACCOMMODATION.

NO OFFICIAL INVESTIGATION INTO THE ACCIDENT WHICH HE CLAIMS TO BE SUPER-VISING HAS EVER BEEN AUTHORISED, NOR SEEMS LIKELY TO BE. THE FINDINGS OF THE FATAL ACCIDENT ENQUIRY HAVE FULLY SATISFIED US THAT, FOR REASONS UNKNOWN, THE PILOTS OF ALPHA WHISKY AND HOTEL CHARLIE TOOK OFF IN THE HOURS OF DARKNESS FROM THE DROME HOTEL AIRSTRIP AND NEVER RETURNED. THE WRECKAGE OF HOTEL CHARLIE WAS DISCOVERED CLOSE TO THE HOTEL IN THE MORNING. BOTH PILOT AND WRECKAGE OF

ALPHA WHISKY COULD NOT BE FOUND BUT FOUR MONTHS LATER THE REMAINS OF THE PILOT WERE FOUND INDICATING HE DIED WITHIN SEVERAL HOURS OF TAKE OFF (POSSIBLY AFTER MIDNIGHT AND DURING THE EARLY HOURS) BUT THE CAUSE OF DEATH WAS EXPOSURE AND NOT IMPACT, AND THAT HIS BODY WAS FOUND ON 96-METRE HILL LESS THAN A MILE FROM THE AIRFIELD IN A STATE OF DECOMPOSITION COMMENSURATE WITH HIS HAVING LAIN, UNDISCOVERED THERE, APART FROM SCAVENGING ANIMALS, FOR THAT PERIOD OF TIME.

THE RECENT DISCOVERY OF AIRCRAFT WRECKAGE IN 90 FEET OF WATER 500 YARDS FROM THE SHORE DOES NOT NECESSITATE INVOLVEMENT OF THE A.A.I.B. OF THE BOARD OF TRADE. AFTER THIS GREAT PASSING OF TIME THE REMAINING WRECKAGE WOULD BE UNLIKELY TO YIELD ANY ANSWERS: THE NIGHT CIRCUIT THESE PILOTS MADE WAS BOTH ILLEGAL AND HIGHLY DANGEROUS. IT IS PATENTLY OBVIOUS THE AIRCRAFT TOUCHED OR COLLIDED ON APPROACH.

AS PUBLIC FUNDS ARE INVOLVED, THE LIFT-ING OF THIS WRECKAGE (OR ANY TYPE OF INVESTIGATION, WHEN, TO PROFESSIONALS

THERE ARE ONLY FOREGONE CONCLU-
SIONS TO BE MADE) COULD NOT BE JUSTI-
FIED BY THE BRANCH.

I FEEL THE . . .

The paper was growing shiny in the metallic light; I lowered
it to my thigh. The girl was smiling at me. 'Brotherhood tells
me you have no money, not a penny, he realised early on. He
also . . .'

She burst out laughing, turned aside and laughed into the
tarpaulin. Colour had come into her cheeks and I noticed her
laughs drew vapour in the cold, damp air. 'He also says you
are completely . . . completely *mad*!' she opened her eyes
wide. 'He says he thinks you've escaped from an institution,
that you're some kind of schizothingmy and you're not who
you think you are, and . . .' she let out big hiccups of laughs,
then she screamed and hit her foot down in a stamp to stop
herself sucking back the laughs . . . 'Says you think Brotherhood has . . . something, says you think Brotherhood has,
broken pieces off . . . off a fucking spaceship!' she flung a
hand up to her mouth and put a finger in between the teeth.
She glared at me. 'And you say I should listen to you!'

'Brotherhood lets me stay because I amuse him . . .'

'Who are you, Mister?'

'I'm an outlier who's come into the circle.'

'You're a liar . . .'

'Oh *piss* off.'

'No you piss off with your advice. Yous are all neurotic,
I'm staying.'

'You listen here and listen good, you go put a flower on your mummy's grave. Get out on the first bus in the morning.'

She slapped down the tarpaulin and screamed at me, 'Don't you get it? Stop telling me what to do!'

I started walking away, 'And I only like Beethoven,' I lied wildly. I turned back and pointed at Carlton's small headstone. 'While you're at it, stick a daisy on that one.'

Evening.

I moved through the lighting-up sections of corridor, towards Brotherhood's victory and my own ration of defeat that was nothing new.

In the Observation Lounge she was already there, perched on a stool, wearing the short skirt Brotherhood had bought for her that morning and she had shortened around the hem, sitting by the log fire all afternoon watching the herons stalk and cross the white horizon beyond the runway. Her legs were like long splashes from a bucket and two husbands were actually leaning against the bar talking to her. I laughed in her face: the last refuge of desperate men. I marched to my table.

Who knows or cares what I ordered and transported to my mouth. *My mouth: one day a glut of dark blood will jerk up into my throat and finish my latest babbling, mid-sentence. I will rake and spit out a clot only to have another one rise up within me, like a birth.*

Brotherhood crossed to my table. He laughed, placed my favourite whisky with crushed ice on the table, 'She's had a fine idea already: a party to liven this old hotel up – a DJ, but a party with a difference. We'll open up the dining room, eh? *All* guests will attend, so don't go hanging yourself before.'

By the time the Observation Lounge smelled of coffee, the young woman had finished eating and returned to the bar where she told stories to two couples, drank a chain of lemonades with fresh orange and was the life of the party; cardigan wrapped round her, leaning back on her stool she shook some hair away from a bare shoulder, the curve of which then reflected the log-fire flames. Brotherhood leaned on the bar encouraging the conversation, prodding it in various directions. Then the couples sheepishly and unwillingly made themselves leave the fun in the name of this new concept called: their marriage. The men had been trying to look at their wives as much as the girl but they hadn't succeeded. I left before the girl and Brotherhood crossed to the flames of the log fire. I sighed, infinitely weary. When I stood up the girl gave me a challenging look. I couldn't bear to hear his patter begin; his tired old routines: revolution, irony, Africa, duality and the uses of black magic rituals at the moment of death; atrocities in the Middle Ages: how they would build little wooden boxes round victims' heads then throw them down the cliffs of the castle; the social position of skull stackers in the Khmer Rouge.

'Goodnight!'

'Nighty night,' they called wickedly, I saw her flat canvas shoes that made her look so young, that summer.

In full view of them I picked up one of the ashtrays. In the reception I didn't push open the fire doors and move up the flickering corridor but I swung out the front door then walked over the gravel of the turning place, round the corner and moved into the pine plantation where, in the dry night, over to the left, I saw honeymoon couples embrace. I stepped into the suddenly-lush beds of chicken weed, over to the patio of 15 and cast the heavy ashtray through the door. Shattering near the bottom, the upper section hesitated then, in a collapse, the glass fell downwards. I laughed out loud, turning to make sure the couple (from 7) saw me. They scuttled off to tell Brotherhood who would nod solemnly but laugh out loud as soon as they'd turned their backs on him.

Morning: 1. Glaziers from the island's other side.
2. A mildness in the sudden air that brought a daddy-long-legs as frail as the filaments in a bulb.
3. Her perfume bottle banging down on the dresser through the wall from my headboard.
4. The poster in the foyer.

Drag Party

8pm Friday night

The Dining Room

Music!

Hot Chilli!

Beer!

All guests must attend

All guests must dress as members of the opposite sex

No excuses — spoilsports

By Order of the Management

JOHN BROTHERHOOD

Editor's note: Argyll Archipelago Records press release glued into manuscript:

NO FANS

High School dance band famed for cover versions of *You Can't Touch This* (MC Hammer) & *You're a Million* (The Raincoats). My first band

LOAMING SCOUNDREL
Drums

DJ CORMORANT
bass

RUFUS TWANG
vocals/congas

DONALD 'DON' MACDONALD
guitar

Rumoured to have gone to University

Scoundrel emigrated to the Central Belt where he found success on the stool of hart-metal band **Excluder!** Played on their first album *'Draft Excluder'* (Leprosy 66666)

THE EARS OF SPOCK

Made their auspicious debut, midsummer night at Clashnessie caravan site

CALUM HOFF
guitar+synth

DJ CORMORANT
bass+fx pedals

RUFUS TWANG
vocals

McNEIL of BARRA
drums

Defected from **THE THROBS** thrash band

Band famed for Hoff's ability to play only the same guitar solo on every song still some great original material and (1) single *Dancing About Architecture* (Vinyl Archipelago 001) which someone in London bought. When offered a year-long residency as show band on the late-night ferry Psalm 23 to the Outer Islands, **THE EARS OF SPOCK** accepted to find McNeil of Barra suffered from chronic seasickness and was frequently replaced, mid-set, by a drum machine after he'd vomited over his kit. When I was spotted, by Mary herself, during a crossing in a gale, vomiting yet not missing a beat on my bass she asked me to join her band.

THE AFTERNOON DAINTIES

CALUM HOFF
guitar

RUFUS TWANG
vocals

McNEIL of BARRA
drums

The **Dainties** moved to Aluminiumville and were regularly bottled off with their brand on indie-pop. Finally disintegrated in a welter of sheep abuse and Lorne sausage overdose allegations.

DJ Cormorant

DIESEL MARY AND HER AIR BRAKES

'KRELL' MacKRELL
guitar

BOB KINZER
keyboards

DJ CORMORANT
electronics/bass

DIESEL MARY
vocals

FOUR-FOUR McBRNON
drums

Hard rocking blues/soul revue (they thought) so when I started feeding in tape loops on the national tour! Recorded live cassette, *'Roof-of-the-Mouth-Mucus and Seven Sunrises'* at the Tighnabruaich Progressive Music Festival when we didn't sleep for a week then went on-stage, everyone started a different song simultaneously, the missing-in-action husband appeared back in the Port with Mary's eight children. The first lady of blues came off the road. Highlight of the national tour was the encore (2ndЩ) at Barcaldine Village Hall, where Mary was so drunk she pissed her knickers and got an electric shock off the mike. I quit singing! I leave the mainland for the island.

THE POST-HUMP HICCUPS

'KRELL' MACRELL
guitar

DJ CORMORANT
bass/vocals

KNIFEGRINDER
drums/vocals

Doing well with our first infamous single: Blow Job From a Virgin (Nala 122) when our drummer discovered a heart condition and began talking about aliens a lot. After the split I concentrate on DJ-ing more. Recorded our unreleased album 'The Fire Escapes Are Burned to Hell' then formed...

THE VICARS OF WAKEFIELD

'KRELL' MACRELL
guitar

JOE THE COAL
bass vocals

BOB KINZER
keyboards

FOUR-FOUR McGINNON
keyboards

Never join a splinter group we should tell our grandchildren. The Vic's followed me onto the island, partly to try and persuade me to rejoin them. Looking back it would've been the natural move. The Vics couldn't get a gig, not even in Wakefield. Meanwhile I had started rehearsing with Thundertown. I was living in a caravan with no electric, me and Marine Girl, the singer in **MUFTI.** The Vics split and, homeless, had to return to Mainland apart from local recruit Joe.

THE BIG WET KNEE

THUNDERTOWN
guitar/vocals

DJ CORMORANT
bass

MARINE GIRL
backing vocals

OLLIE McMABOLE
guitar

THE ARGONAUT
drums

Legendary Strat player, Thundertown, rehearsed his band for seven months and we had one of the best, if craziest, drummers around (he filled his tom toms with sea-water). Thundertown was half Red Indian, Cherokee or something like that; he came back after the Tracking Station shut. We got to rehearsing in the old fire station at Far Places and the first gig was to be in The Summer Colony. Thundertown had arranged it so we would be flown in using Nam's helicopter. Real class arrival, but Argonaut had let me wire up his entire drum set with wah-wah pedals. I was a bit out of it on a tasty mix of Kativril pills, a bottle of coffee liqueur and half a can of Carnation milk and a whole bottle of brandy with brown sugar in it; Yummy. Thundertown freaked when he heard what I'd done and I was sacked, replaced with Walter Greinger-Smith a twelve-year-old musical prodigy who learned all my bass lines in the afternoon and played them faultlessly. I decided to quit and concentrate on a sound system and my own music. I'd been blown away by Guy (called Gerald's, Voodoo Ray and was more into dance music, mixing up early Ultravox, Be-Bop Deluxe with drum machines and old Rwanda. Incidentally, Thundertown was so wasted at the gig, Walter Greinger had to step over and switch off the effects pedals for him.

McMabole went on to produce Bert Drrivens' ceilidh band. Last heard of on outer islands in Gaelic super-group **ARMANI SUITS.**

DJ CORMORANT'S *LACERATION FETISH SOUND SYSTEM*

DJ CORMORANT
electronics

MARINE GIRL
vocals/electronics

In our small, hand-built studio we recorded two long (12) singles that Argyll Archipelago have put out: Flashing Squares and an underground hit, The Weeping Blisters of Job, that brought in enough money for me to try and promote a few dance events on the island.

FIRST TEXT
Part Two

'**S**ome of them are condoms!' a honeymooner-couple-man called and right enough, some of the balloons on the ceiling of the never-used dining room – stuck up round the fakey chandeliers with pale surgical tape from Brotherhood's father's skinny wrists where his glucose drips fitted into him – some of those fixed-up balloons *were* Durexes.

It was DJ Cormorant who DJ'd the drag party and then grew in him desires to organise millennial rave after that Christmas: to celebrate advents of new centuries.

He was out the portico bawling, 'May all your landings be gentle,' as the tippy-up back of Joe the Coal's lorry dumped the metal-cornered bass bins.

Still dressed as man, Brotherhood appeared at dusk with a box of records, but it was all Bob Dylan. I went for a walk down past the airfield gate, grass soaking the canvas shoes, across open spaces that would fill with marquees, DJs and tribesters at Hogmanay. Then I saw the familiar figure haunting per usual hinterlands of Drome Hotel: The One Who Walked the Skylines of Dusk with Debris Held Aloft Above His Head. His long black raincoat, like an office worker's in a city, foreshadowed the lyrics of Dylan's Man in the Long Black Coat – a song I would circle to in his arms that night (my fingers on the bare flesh of the man's neck, above his dress's low-cut back) – one of the many scratched, mysterious waltzes Brotherhood had indicated as the only permissible music.

The raincoat was slapping about his legs as he lurched, madly measuring out distances halfway up the runway; looking into sky then with a lone, still-headed stare out to the Sound waters where his unattainable aircraft lay all-sunken, he made a note in a wee book.

It was getting dark when I saw the Aircrash Investigator turn against the last slick of light upon the wide waters; he seemed to take a long look in my direction. It was then I spotted the figure between us, head slumped down and moving at a walking pace, though I couldn't see the feet, just he/she making *its* way forth where banking of the ground beyond the runway dips down to stony shore. As you watched you guessed the new figure was three hundred yards-ish distant, legs hidden by sheaves of moor grass. It came closer, in the half-light, harder to distinguish it from darkshadow where the jetty began. The Aircraft Investigator in his blackcoat began to point, I could see him show his erect arm to the first stars: it wasn't at me he was pointing but the walking figure. The Aircrash Investigator shook both hands in the air so you recognised he had started running. Then I turned my head, but as my eyes adjusted, as close as I would ever see, the ghost's head still bowed, movements stiff and face so pale it seemed blue-coloured: no feet, spookily floating along the stones.

I heard a sound; at first I thought it was a seagull then I recognised the humanness of a shout: The Coated One Who Walked the Skylines was waving me, calling me. I frowned, sudden, in coldness offof what I'd seen. I walked towards him across the runway but he veered down the shore banking out of sight. By the time I'd crossed, Aircrash Investigator was along under the seaweed covered jetty-supports (the tide was right out); the other figure was nowhere to be seen. I squinted shore darkness and open runway space but the ghost was gone.

'I hear a kangaroo has escaped from the zoo now,' gasped out the coated guy, arms chucked out to balance, one leg so bended at the knee; the slope so steep his face almost touched the grass. He chuckled, hard.

'Aye. So I heard. They took the grizzly away slung under the helicopter,' I says.

He nodded, looked both ways then leaned his palms on his knees. The belt of the overcoat had come loose of its loops, the grass had saturated it so wet it was glisteny as it dragged and suddenly gave me such powerful (what I call privately) Human-Frailty feelings for the leaned-over man. I almost blurted out everything. Tears came bubbling out and I wanted to dish a big hug on him. Human Frailty, never to be confused with the thing called pity; I was only saved by his excited blethers.

'You were so close and you saw it, eh?'

I nodded, my eyes bright below the tripping skies that were starting to shuffle in plains of stars.

'Like you've seen a ghost. Hey, help me out. I've got to get dressed, there's no woman among all these wives I can ask . . .'

As we walked up to the hotel, away from the ghost-sighting, in darkness now, One Who Walks the Skylines of Dusk says of how days had passed 'as they do'. He mentioned Chef Macbeth's buzzing remote-control aircraft 'circling through these unbearable afternoons' and, the phrase I like best, 'the couples who linger like graveyard statues in the pine plantation.'

In his room he says to me, 'I may as well be Robinson Crusoe.'

'Tonight I'll be your *Man* Friday,' I smiled. He roared in the hystericals, returned the long-forgotten-about raincoat to the empty wardrobe. From the suitcase (behind it an almost empty bottle of Spar whisky) he took the suit. I held the jacket with my fingers then swung it on, pulling it tight onto my sides by pushing arms straight into the bottoms of pockets. He had covered the mirrors of his room with towels long ago so I moved to the bathroom shouting, 'Do you have a shirt?' realising that never before would he have heard a voice calling from there.

So in a once-elegant suit gathered around my feet he saw my socks still on, my fingernails with titchy remains of coloured Miss Selfridge's nail varnish. It was then he began to realise.

He said, 'You won't show me your feet, cause of new nail varnish. I smashed your window; you must've been afraid, if only I'd realised before,' he laughed, 'you're amazing, just amazing. You didn't come to me to lay those two dresses on the bed and try to win the Belle of the Ball, you didn't come to show me the few bits of make-up and lipstick you filched from the youngest-looking two of all the wives, or to show me how to measure my foundation shade against the blue veins of my wrist,' he says, 'you want to show me you and I are the same, you've come to reveal the truth. At first I thought it was . . .'

When he'd got me to take off the woolly, itchy socks from the Chandlers we stared at each other. I put down the Ladyshave, says, 'I'll call for you at quarter-to; get *your* legs shaved!' and headed out wearing his suit.

An hour later I'm walking with him, arm-in-arm up the corridor; a honeymoon couple were in front: the man's muscled thighs beneath a short skirt, the woman's hair brylcreemed back, a lit cigarette in her hand that she wasn't smoking.

More of the bizarre drag couples were gathered in the dining room, laughing and admiring each other's clothes. DJ Cormorant, looking glum behind his mixing desk, droning out Dylan, a whelk-picker's halogen lamp bouncing up and down as he perused Brotherhood's circled tracks on The Permitted Albums.

Chef Macbeth, dressed as a nurse, was serving draught beer from behind the white-clothed buffet table far across the dining room. Everywhere the men-figures were lifting half pints or soft drinks to their mouths; the women-figures were guzzling pints and staining whisky glasses with bright red lipstick. A man-figure in a sailor suit holding a life-belt came in with a woman figure shoving out a massive bosom that parted the doors; the woman was Shan the Ferryman, the man was his wife.

A woman-figure in seventeenth-century high white wig with tumbles of sparkling earrings stepped in, looked around. Through the viciously applied foundation I recognised Brotherhood; the velvet of his dress shifted as he crossed and spoke sharply to Macbeth, lifted a clutched pint to his pale face.

Mrs Heapie entered with her husband. She'd really gone to town with an orange boilersuit buffed up with oil stains, a construction worker's hard-hat and a menacing big monkey-wrench that she placed, carefully, down on the tablecloth, her steel-toed boots sparkled gaily in the disco lights.

And I, One Who Walked the Skylines on my arm, I'd gone and drawn a man-moustache, *bigote*, above my lips with curly ends; the baggy suit and my titchy canvas shoes. The One Who Walked had one of the wives' (from 12 I think) short dresses showing his long, now smooth, legs but we hadn't been able to get him fitting shoes, so's at the end of those great legs were just the clodhopper boots but we waltzeyd straight off to that Father of Night Dylan track (1:29) (How mysterious, containing all things that are hidden.)

When we'd done our little dance, saying, 'Time for medicine,' Aircrash Investigator moved towards Macbeth, far across the dance floor.

I knew the way people's eyes jumped a little looking at it, my moustache moved funny when I did the talking. 'What's with the music?' I says to Cormorant who we'd all known of once, on account of his always playing in bands.

'It's Brotherhood's.'

I kneeled and flicked through the every one of Dylan's albums.

'Fancy some hash?' Cormorant says.

'Nah,' I went.

'You're cute, even as a guy; how about it?'

'Get lost.'

'Is that your husband?'

'Nut.'

Cormorant nodded, the light swishing on his forehead. Then, saddest of everything, he played Sign on the Window; we looked a long time then, ever so gingerly, smiled at the beautiful sadness.

Brotherhood strode up with more drag couples. He was chortling but I saw through the smile how he was spying on me and the Investigator for as to what was up. Brotherhood walked to me and tapped his breasts upwards with the palms of his hands, 'I'm unpacking'.

The Aircrash Investigator stepped over as I rose from the box of records with Permitted Tracks on them.

'I wish you were a man. I'd ask you to dance,' says Aircrash Investigator to Brotherhood.

'Oh we can double up: I'm *very* open-minded.'

'You look lovely,' I says, so they two wouldn't maybe fight.

'How about a kiss, Mister?' asked Brotherhood.

'I don't want lipstick on my collar,' I goes.

Both men, in their women-clothes, laughed. I leaned to Brotherhood's earring and whispered, 'I'm not afraid of you.'

'Mmm,' he went, thoughtfully.

DJ Cormorant shouted, 'Hey Mister Bro'hood, Mr Bro'hood Dude, this stuff is sharp, lyrically I'm talking about, but I could really fuck everyone up if I mixed in a few breakbeats. I mean, these fiddles, they're de*pressing* man — the fiddle's unsexy, like the trombone.'

Without looking over at the DJ, Brotherhood says, 'Just you play what I told you — and whatever, save I'll Be Your Baby Tonight until last; here . . .'

Brotherhood grabbed the microphone.

'Ladies and Gentlemen — or should I say Gentlemen and Ladies — I, and all of us here at Drome Hotel, thank you for joining in so spiritedly. Chilli and rice is being served by Nurse Macbeth, with beer to keep everything from getting too steamy. A contest for the beau and belle of the ball will be held later but meanwhile will you all please take the floor for a waltz.'

'Get it *on*, man,' Brotherhood hissed.

DJ Cormorant started spinning the song: a lolloping, weird waltz with fiddles and harmonicas called Isis.

The couples started grabbing each other's drag-dressed wives and husbands. Suddenly, Brotherhood lifted my hands then waltzed me out into the middle of the floor. He waltzed dead well, while he mouthed the lyrics of Isis at my face as if he was trying to communicate something. As I listened to the words I learned I could make Brotherhood my victim.

The One Who ... etc ... The Debris Man, looked toward us. Watching him over Brotherhood's velvet shoulder I saw him hitch up the bosom then begin to cross towards Macbeth who saw his advance and looked down, worried, at the beer he was pouring. Straight away The Debris Man was round and dragging Macbeth onto the dance-floor. In his nurse uniform, Chef Macbeth tried to laugh it off but yous could tell the amount furiousness he had, all pent up in him. Yous could tell the Aircrasher was getting his own back as he squeezed their big breasts to each other and made Macbeth circle much faster than normal in an over-the-top waltz. The Aircrasher stopped and spun Macbeth round with his legs rising off the ground helplessly. The nurse's skirt rumpled up, giving the sickening sight of the chef's splotchy legs gripped in fishnet stockings.

Other drag-couples waltzed, cheered and showed the gumption enough to stand aside as Macbeth turned all the faster then was suddenly flung aside, hit the wood tiles and rolled the once. Macbeth straight-away shot up on his feet but one of his high heels buckled under him and he sat down.

Brotherhood had to stop the dancing with me cause of his hysterics, he was rubbing his make-up into a complete soup. Another waltz called Winterlude started, so I crossed to Aircrasher who was at the tap himself, serving beer under frowns from Mrs Heapie, her monkey wrench at hand as she served out dollops of ferocious chilli con carne with rice.

Brotherhood helped Macbeth to his feet, shouted at him and tottered over, his wig knocked to one side.

Houlihan, Man Who Walked the Skylines – whatever – with his Irishish name, passed a paper plate of chilli speared with plastic fork. 'Get that down the middle of your neck,' he goes.

I took one taste and got pins and needles in my face. 'Jesus,' I says, reached out and took a hold of his big pint for a wolfing of a few gulps.

We waltzed again, hand on his smooth shiny shoulder, his bare arms around the material of his own suit.

'The ghost,' he whispered.

'We saw it,' I nodded.

'Together,' he goes.

DJ Cormorant put a boogie-ish number on: Down Along the Cove. Crazy Brotherhood, owner of the whole sheboogle, led in a hokey-kokey; a lot of chests and asses got put in, taken out and shaken all about: more than some busts could be expected to endure, and there was a rash of collapsications and shifting bra adjustings. Then Brotherhood was organising and led a conga line – even us and DJ Cormorant having to do the joining in as we wove out the dining-room doors and off up and down the corridor, lighting the rooflights first-time-ever all the ways down. The length of the line came, twisting a bit clumsy-like, out of rhythm up the spiral staircase, round the Observation Lounge: some of the rear-line figures holding beer bottles they'd swiped, passing the bar, those tanning the bottles and eventually dropping them on the dining-room floor where feet went on kicking and spinning them round on the shiny dancing tiles.

Brotherhood, me and the man stood beside the DJ Cormorant's desk, Brotherhood's fake jewels sparkling.

'You're really getting into your parts, guys,' DJ Cormorant nodded.

The Aircrash Investigator goes, 'Hey, son, your baseball cap's on the wrong way round.'

'Ho ho. Bro'hood, Sir. What we were talking about: the mainer. Big one after Christmas to bring in all the piller kiddies. Perfect pitch down on the airfield.'

'What's this?' I goes.

'Repetitive beats from amplified systems. That's where the money is at the end of *this* century. You guys make the misery, you guys may as well muscle in on the escapism from it.'

'I'm thinking of expanding. Drugs.' Brotherhood nodded firmly.

'Not just drugs, Mr Bro'hood, the entire holistic escapist theme park right here at Drome Hotel and its environs. I can engineer it for you.'

'How does that sound to you, children?' Brotherhood smiled and placed a hand on our shoulders. He added, 'I'll handle security.'

A lump chilli con carne flew through the air, splattered on some man's hairy, bare back, just below the effulgence of his imitation diamond clasp.

DJ leaned forward to try protect the decks as more blobs of chilli came slowly arcing, sailing across close to the ceiling. A stray lump, thrown by some man in an imitation fur coat, soared over and hit a stumbling girl wearing a false beard that seemed of cotton wool.

Crouched by the DJ's desks I saw it all: the young wife

who'd lent me Aircrasher's dress – and the Rimmel stuff – marched forward, cradling a huge kitchen pot, her brand new husband in the blue dress (darkened on the thigh by direct hits) at her side. She clawed fists into the pot and flung bracelets of chilli ahead. Men? women? roared and men screamed as blood-red gashes of chilli opened up, glossy on the lacy clothes and pale faces – surely both those men felt at home in this feast of wet wounds? A spatter caught the Aircrash Investigator on his smooth bare chest just above cleavage. He stepped forward and heaved the pot away from the dressed-as-a-golfer-girl, plunged his hand and ground a load into the girl's face who screamed. The husband slammed a gateau into the Aircrasher's face. That halted him for a tick as his eyes opened up through synthetic cream then Aircrasher lifted the pot and tipped the full load over the husband who tried to dodge but, in his high heels, couldn't move sharply enough – a huge glut of chilli sauce slid down his bare back and brushed the sticking-out-arse as it plopped to the floor, a high heel jerked out to one side leaving a clear strip of wood flooring: the guy was down as Aircrash Investigator stepped over him dropping the pot with a clang.

Chilli and gateau were flying everywhere. 'Follow me, stick by my side,' called the Investigator. A handful of chilli hit my face and my eye began to sting like fury but with the other I saw enough to weed my way through all – towards Brotherhood who leaned, tossing out plates of chilli, wig awry, like some terrible aircrash victim, blood-thick sauce strewn down him like mutilation. Aircrash Investigator punched with all his weight and caught Brotherhood below the eye. I winced as the wig flew off, pale powdered face highlighted under still-sandy hair. Brotherhood landed on his arse, legs out, wet hairs twisted and compressed under the revolting stockings. The Aircrasher's face slapped aside by a hit of chilli.

The room had divided into two camps: one sheltering behind the buffet tables, the other salvaging and returning dollops of chilli from the wailing DJ's desk. I was caught in the crossfire of No Man's Land.

'Follow me,' the Aircrash Investigator says.

We both dropped to our knees. Casualties, drunk – and a couple not officially man and wife, together snogging, lay among the red puddles of sauce.

As the Aircrasher, Warmer, One Who Walked Skylines . . . Monsieur Debris . . . all the names he used on me then . . . as he took my hand and we crawled together out of that dining room, DJ Cormorant jumped up and down, clapping gallantly: the sound system began blasting I'll Be Your Baby Tonight.

SECOND MANUSCRIPT
Part Two

What must have happened back in my room is: I said to her,
'If you take off your shoes and socks, I'll be able to see you're
the same as me.'

She stood in my ruined last suit, reached up to remove a
kidney-bean skin from her neck. I looked at the speckles of
nail varnish on the ends of the fingers. I said, 'At first I
thought it was because you had lost everything when the wee
ferry sunk, then I realised you wouldn't put up with
Brotherhood's humiliations, the clothes he bought you,
unless, well unless you were broke. I lay awake trying to
imagine why you put up with it till I realised you had no
choice. This is why, if you take off your shoes and socks I
think we'll see you've put nail varnish on your toes; you
haven't put it on your fingers because that would be too
obvious, the nail varnish of these young wives is the first
make-up you could get hold off since you got here.

I took out my bra and padding.

She nodded and sat on the end of the bed.

Finally she said, 'Do you think he'll get the police?'

I laughed, looked at her.

'Ahm, I've to get a shower,' she shrugged, stood. 'It was wrong to hit him. It was . . . Mmm. Too early. He'll chuck you out. Then I'll be alone here. Though there is a one up on the hill above who's keeping watch on us, he might let you stay in his tent. There again, he might not.'

'He won't.' I thought of the Devil's Advocate, lying now in the darkness, on the elevated horizontal larch, the same one Carlton died across; the Devil's Advocate would lie surrounded by the amphibious blacks of moon-glazed puddles in the slap-wet lands, glaring up at warbles of starlight; the rifle or semi-automatic, or verge cutter recently sharpened by the travelling Knifegrinder, clawed to his fat chest, sloping downwards so blade or muzzle rests beneath his chin as he waits, bides his time to stir from his lair and come down into the enclosures around the hotel.

At nine o'clock in the morning I heard the brass bell on the reception desk ring down in the foyer below. The farce of her departure had begun and the dusty irritation of the unused bell was a great touch on her part, anything to deepen the claws in the flesh of the morning; anything that allowed us to use the props and stage scenery around us, in this folly of plaster and wood panelling on subsiding muck.

Brotherhood with a blue and yellow black eye was behind the bar, serving bacon rolls to the hardier of the honeymoon couples, but as he calmly folded the dish-towel and gave me a challenging glance, he also noted the witnesses around him. I was on my feet before he rounded the bar.

'Morning,' I said, halfway down the spiral staircase, then I crossed to the neglected pot of ivy where I leaned with the bright sun behind me.

The girl stood at the desk with the kitbag leaning against her leg. I reached up and chipped at something caught in the curves of my left ear: a little piece of dried, almost black, chilli sauce came away. (When I'd showered the night before, half kidney beans lay in the plughole.)

Brotherhood walked round, behind her then took up position at the desk. The air radio burbled with the frequency of some high airliner heading across the Atlantic, miles above us.

'Checking out?' he squeaked, so cheerily his bruised face must have hurt him.

The girl moved her head the once.

'Now, room 15.' Brotherhood produced the thin paper chit I would look at in the afternoon with the numerals £665 written at the bottom.

'I have no money,' said the young woman.

'Pardon?' Brotherhood rolled his eyes and smiled.

For the benefit of the now-attentive, newly married and supposedly self-absorbed ears above, the girl repeated, 'I have no money; around seventeen pence down in the lining of my old jacket.'

'Ah, and you intend to post me the money when you reach your destination?' he raised his eyebrows, virtually as if reading from an auto-cue positioned out on the sunny gravel through the dirty glass behind me.

Now, gambling everything on those instincts as to what he would do — perhaps even sharp enough in those days to see all that lay before us, she said, 'I have no destination.'

'In that case how do you intend to make good your debt?'

'Could I no do some dishes?'

Brotherhood swole out his bottom lip and with his fingers, pretending he couldn't recall the figure there, turned the chit slowly so it faced him. 'Mmm-uh,' he mused, lifted up the bit of paper, leaned over and, so it must have made contact with her left breast, he snugly rustled the paper into the little front pocket that hung on the man's shirt she was wearing. 'Follow me,' he said and walked towards the front door; stylishly, so I wasn't expecting it, without looking at me he muttered, 'You too.'

Macbeth's junk was piled outside in the sunshine and he was transporting it through the paths of the pine plantation to the far end of the room extensions using a cement-stained wheelbarrow.

'On you go Macbeth, son, no more damp transistors for you, room 16. You two can fight among yourself what one you want, they're both rotten. You can work on your self-loathing together out here. Thank me that summer's coming.'

'Brotherhood,' I said, 'My work?'

'What work!' he shouted. 'Jesus Christ, man, I prefer the freedoms of my dreamscapes as well, but you're crazy.' He looked at the girl; repeated, 'He's crazy: Japan, Boeing, tensile steels; he's lying, all an extension of the rubbish you tell inquisitive barbers in a city you'll never return to . . . such a bullshit artist it's coming out his collar.' He laughed and strode away shouting as he went, 'you can have showers when there's a spare room if no one is moving in. Macbeth'll show you the ropes in the kitchen and you,' he pointed to the girl, 'Can have a shot at changing those new marital sheets every morning.'

One hour later the girl and I were flitted to our respective caravans. Sat on the back-breaking cot, running my palms over the bristles appearing on my shins I could hear the thumps and creaks as she moved around next door, pathetically arranging her few things in order.

Wednesday the Eleventh

The purple bruises of bluebell banks had begun to appear on the slopes above the hotel.

I moved in through the fake Mexican portico, the morning walk from my caravan marking the distance that was set up, in a revolutionary manner, between myself, the girl and our former fellow-diners up in the Observation Lounge, each couple unable to assimilate the sudden inversion of status that had taken place, aware that such revolutions could be lurking for them in life ahead.

When I moved out to the caravan I had nothing to take. A few tunes clanged around my brainbox, a few worn shoes and shirts are all I've left the world to remember me by, but I've learned something, she is better than this world, better.

I walked beneath the balcony, hearing the moronic, frenzied clicking of cereal plates. Smiling, enduring the latest shatting from fate, I heaved in the kitchen swing-doors, saw the sluice of light that came in the horizontal window slits, saw the dishes she had stacked after dinners the night before, saw the cheerful, colourful wires, sprouting from the rear of the new and un-fitted deep-fat frier.

She would have been upstairs since eight a.m. in the new, short skirt and thick-weave stockings and the jumper she insisted on wearing: all of which Brotherhood loved to call 'Your uniform'. She would be serving the breakfast buffet, mainly just tea and coffee.

I removed the large butter chunk from the fridge and put it down by the butter-cube cutter. I lifted the two aluminium securing pins and the cast top then dropped the butter chunk into the casing. I replaced the top, re-fitted the securing pins then, using both hands, slowly but firmly turned the handle. The screw would be pushing the butter chunk up against the end of the casing where two small holes with serrated edges squeezed the butter out in long, drooping poles which were severed by a wire, turned in unison by the compressing handle. The severed butter cubes plopped into a Pyrex bowl of water.

When I'd squeezed in the block I returned the bowl to the fridge after tipping in a tray of ice cubes. I crossed to the deep and hateful old sink, shaped with dents and bevels, turned the hot tap – so deep that she, with her straight back, was almost unable to reach it with a pink, rubber glove. I filled the peeled-grey plastic sink with scalding water and then cooled it with cold. When I placed the parts of the butter-cube maker in the basin, archipelagos of iridescence floated when the bubbles of cheap washing-up liquid dissolved.

The kitchen held in a sweet odour of butchers' shops on a summer's day: the same sweetness as when the rows of shoes, their grips caked with meaty chilli sauce had been put out for cleaning all along the corridor. (Brotherhood had taken the lot over to Laundromat Blues at Far Places, put all the footwear in a washing machine then stood with his back against the door of the tumble dryer as the shoes crashed around.)

Fresh from my old room Macbeth walked in and nodded to the tattie sack.

'Aye-aye,' I said.

The girl entered from the side door and started clearing the clean dishes from the sinkside.

'Three-pan Macbeth, do you have to use a different pot each time you do scrambled eggs?'

'You just bend your arse. To the work. And you, tattie-hoiker.'

I heaved the bag over to the sink and began lifting tatties under the ice-cold stream of tap-water, thumbing the clayey coin-sized mud from the white and pink flesh. I dropped the cleaned with a bang in the sink.

The girl looked over at me. I carried the clean potatoes to the peeler, tipped them in from the basin and to shut off Macbeth who was sneering, I jerked the switch that started vibrating the potatoes around the sandpapery interior.

'Don't think yous can lord it over me . . .'

Late, after dinners, the sound of her coming back to her caravan: she will be breathing in deep the real poverty of these lands, but breathing at a controlled speed, with which she's learned to steady despair and not allow it to swarm over her, like a cluster of orange fish eggs clinging to the lens of sunglasses – as in some of her most recent nightmares which she mentions to me when we sit on Schweppes crates at her caravan door, mild summer rains manoeuvring around the mountains, the position of the Devil's Advocate's new camp visible, her fingers twisting grass-stalks into little balls and tossing them at nothing. She will cover herself with the rugs, the door secured shut with a length of wire. Though I didn't understand then I now know. She will lie looking up at an identical curved ceiling to mine, smiling, biding her time, the borrowed alarm clock ticking beside her.

Mosquito Bite

Competition
Friday 7pm

Topless Competition for Husbands and Wives

Endurance test against our local mosquito,
the midge, entrants must sit topless in
the pine plantation for one hour,
Winner: highest number of bite marks.

First prize £500

JOHN BROTHERHOOD

Another summer came, summers I had once known how to go about loving. The black dot of Macbeth's radio-controlled aircraft climbed higher than ever into the cloudless sky. Across the Sound, peaks that had been invisible all winter became clear in the brilliant distance. Brotherhood mowed the airfield, riding, shirt off, on the machine; honeymoon couples flew in and out, the bright coloured aircraft moved above white froth from the summer ferry as it crossed the Sound several times a day.

In my foolishness, sequestered with the girl in our caravans, her hair tied back because she couldn't wash it that often, wearing the clumsy pullover despite the mildness, Brotherhood's mower buzzing in the distance – in those foolishnesses (as she would say) I almost believed happiness a possibility!

On the evening of the midgie competition the hotel population gathered, some wives and husbands soon retreated to watch the on-going endurance from the Observation Lounge windows.

'No women? No women?' Brotherhood was shouting. He turned to look at the girl who was standing by a tree, disinterested, 'Let me allow you to pay off your debt, lassie.'

She scowled, pasty, as if Macbeth's infinite stodge had filled up her cheeks: it was a teenage glare from beneath dark eyebrows, 'Get bosoms out and driven demented by midgie bites so you can hide up the stair pulling off the gander's head?'

I laughed and a few of the couples nervously tittered. Brotherhood tilted his head, smiling with a terrible mock affection at the girl in her deliberately tawdry jumper.

She's still young; can endure and survive the desolation she's got stuck in temporarily.

'How about our kitchen porter?'

I shrugged and pulled the shirt, the orange, rough-cotton one I still believe belonged to my father, tugging over the head, so even as the collar came free of my ruffled hair my stare was still directed at Brotherhood, who, without breaking the stare, as if we were in some movie that entertained yet still threw around a few noble ideas, thumbed open the buttons down his front and walked towards the centre of the concrete paths.

I also stepped forward where Shan stood with the ropes. Shan had no cigarette in his mouth: he had coated his face in paraffin: Danger of Explosion.

'You're a bunch of spoilsports,' I scowled at the fucking young husbands standing ('stood' as she would say), looking on.

One of the young men piped up, 'He said guests couldn't join in,' and nodded out to Brotherhood.

'Well, I so wanted to play with you and her, this lot might ask a refund if they get bit bad,' Brotherhood placed his hands behind his back and Shan started to tie them. A spray of midges were already blowing around me.

Brotherhood sank to the grass in a lotus position, I copied – facing him. In minutes a mist of little insects cluttered up my nostrils as Shan kneeled, smelling like the hurricane lamp we used to light our hut up in Devil Woods when we played commandos. Shan tied my hands and I sat.

As Shan stood back more midges swarmed about my ears, darted about on my tender, closed eyelids, formed a carpet on my back, raced and tickled and bit across my chest and stomach – where the skin was softest.

I opened my eyes. In the dusk light you could see the living clouds around Brotherhood's naked torso and the head: a circling, dark mask coated his face and I realised mine too must be like that: a black sheet of frothing little lives. I gritted teeth, knowing from experience that you might get furiously bitten, but only the mysterious few exit points of your own blood would blossom into the little pink blotch used in the counting at the end.

You could hear the cringey moans of the remaining and impressively sadistic onlookers, smoking and waving their hands furiously over by the big, oldest pine.

Suddenly I saw Brotherhood's head go back (his eyes open all the time) and the mouth wide – clear red/pink and the draw of white teeth in a dry, cruel laugh – a foul quilt of midges plumed upwards about him then his face fell still, dead-seeming.

When the whistle sounded Shan whacked me with a towel, untied the hands and I rubbed all over me as a cheer came from behind the glass of the panorama window above. Brotherhood raced down to the creosote fence, legged himself over, raced across the runway and down the embanking so he disappeared.

'I saw it,' Brotherhood whispered up in the Observation Lounge. I didn't hear him at first, walked closer; his hair was flattened down with the water and for effect he held a limp sliver of seaweed that touched the orange carpet. His nipples were shrunken in the coldness – couples applauded – he had so many bites they almost conjoined to a single blotch. His lips mumbled so I stepped closer. Several people were talking to him at the same time; he stumbled slightly as Mrs Heapie pushed him to and fro, marking off the bites with felt-tip then Shan notching them in the book.

'Sixty-seven . . . sixty-eight . . .'

Brotherhood moved his mouth near my face, 'I saw him, blue-faced . . .'

Macbeth stuck the pen deep on to my skin as he began the count.

'You saw him?'

'I chucked myself into the seaweed by the jetty, stood up and shook my head, when I turned round he was there, walking away into the vapour. Like you described.'

I nodded sharply, looking sideways to see what my score was.

'Amazing feeling.'

The count was done. The girl left before the figures were announced. It was obvious. Brotherhood had 67 to my 43.

'I could've done with that smash.'

'Oh, don't be ridiculous, you know you can walk out of here when you want.' He was leaned against the bar, shirt on but unbuttoned, its ribbed fronting concertina'd under his arms, 'You're living this farce as I do: I won't call the police, I despise the police; you're enjoying it as much as me, this game, as much as she is. Now,' he started doing up his shirt-front, 'I'm away upstairs to talk to my daddy.'

Thursday the Second. Moon in Capricorn

I was lying in the dark when I heard the girl's steps come across the turning place, muffle for a second behind the (unconnected) gas cylinders, circle my head and pause outside her caravan. I'd noticed that pausing step more and more as summer drove on and the date we must have recompensed Brotherhood was passed beyond and unspeakingly forgotten.

I heard her creakings next door then the sounds of the Knifegrinder's motorcycle advanced up the driveway and I was pulling on trousers, sensing dangers.

I was dismayed the Grinder didn't drive on to the portico but kicked out his bike-stand then killed the engine adjacent to the caravans.

His boots forced their way up to the girl's caravan and he knocked.

'Get lost,' the girl called.

The noise of the boots moved and I tugged open the door that scraped on the uneven floor. I nodded to the man; badges, bits of wire, ring-pulls and some shrivelled fieldmouse creature were fixed to his leather jacket.

'I've found the propeller,' he said.

'Step in.' I smiled at the grizzled man before me. I looked around, at my few belongings, the girl's shining CD that I kept as a solitary ornament to my poverty.

'I'm not interested,' I said.

'What? You says if . . . Look, I don't like coming here at night . . .'

'Oh. Why?'

'The spacemen, man. I even heard Brotherhood saw a ghost here earlier in the summer and he doesn't stop talking about it. It's not a fit site to have a rave, man, cause you can pick up on all the vibes when you're raving, man.'

With my back turned to him I heard him say, 'The propeller is in the Argonaut's house over in The New Projects . . .'

'Keep your voice down,' I said.

'Scorgie the Argonaut, man, used to play drums in The Big Wet Knee. I think he'd give you it for a thousand but I want a ration as well, man. Shit! I shouldn'ty of telt you where it is. I'm a dafty . . .'

'The lassie's trying to sleep.' I fractionally moved my head, 'What time is it?'

He pushed at a digital watch that bleeped, 'Half-two in the morning. I put all my information into this watch, look, look . . . it reads it out, I've got all sorts programmed in here . . .'

I opened the drawer with my passport, driving licence and a single fake Department of Transport claim form, then I shoved the lot in my trouser pocket. *Why not, an absurd final wager. Go through the motions, maybe get some edible food. Should be able to cross it in a night. Really, I've been bored with this for*

months and I don't care about her; she's like all the others. I'd wipe
away the half-hearted pulsation I call love the same way I'd wipe my
sperm off her thigh with a hankie.

'Is that the place on the coast, The New Projects, along from Ferry Slipway?'

'At The Inaccessible Point, the houses there were mainly financed by The Island Society for Encouraging Fisheries but the Argonaut built his own; you'll notice it, oh aye.'

'I'll need to check the prop. How am I to know it's the one?'

'You just remember the Knifegrinder,' he backed out the caravan and wheeled his motorbike off, starting it at the far end of the drive.

Friday the Third. Dawn

So I crossed the mountains. I had no intentions of saying goodbye to the girl. I left the CD on the dew-soft grass outside her caravan, turned my head towards the breeze coming off the Sound. I walked without looking back, climbing away from 96-Metre Hill.

When I reached the Devil's Advocate's camp the fire didn't seem to have been lit for days. The tent was zipped up and sealed with a little padlock you'd use on a case. I took a black, hard piece of wood charcoal to slash the material then tugged it apart. The interior smelled of stale Ritz biscuits. There were a few books. The *Penguin Dictionary of Saints*, *Who Moved The Stone* by Frank Morrison, Aleister Crowley's book of Magickal Correspondences and a copy of *Viz*.

Higher in the hills everything was budding, the trees dotted with the prayer-like, still-enfolded hands of leaves. I could hear the healthy life of water ahead and I was moving through the saplings, turning first this way then that, leaning to avoid the thicker branches.

I slept in the glen the foresters were clearing, in a larch cluster, waking at least every hour. In daylight I walked using my shadow on the ground to judge what horseflies or big insects were buzzing behind me.

Brotherhood had told me how the hillsides were planted: the cannon from the man o' war dragged up and the mountains pounded all day with canister-shot of seeds, spores and cones, 'The hillsides streaked with gunpowder smoke but flowers and shrubs sprouting from that beautiful warfare.'

Afternoon on the second day I came out on the jutting rocks high above The New Projects: there was a cluster of bungalows around a pebbly beach, all looking vulnerable to flood-waters, and further back a lower, longer house skirted by a wall, its roof tiles catching the light. The usual debris of the island lay on the high-tide mark: rusted tanks, nets, creels and skiffs capsized on the grass against the rain. Just offshore were the bright pink and orange dots of mooring buoys. Something else, further out into the water of the bay: on a raft.

I followed the curving path down onto the fenced fields below the trees. It was then I heard the beat – steady and unmistakable with no accompaniment, then the slash of a cymbal: someone playing a drum set.

As I squinted at the horizon where sea met evening sky I saw the flash of a hi-hat. Out on the water floated a small raft with a drum kit on it that must have been nailed down; a man was hunched on a stool playing a steady rock beat. The drum-raft was secured with a long nylon rope to the shore. It tilted slightly in the low swell.

I strolled towards the houses, soon enough recognising the

Argonaut's place. It was surrounded by a waist-height wall: the wall gave off a strange light with the sun behind it and I suddenly realised that the entire construction was made of green and brown beer bottles fixed together with cement. I looked up at the tiles on the roof which also sparked in the afternoon blue – the roof looked like drips of paint had been splattered across – yellow, red, terracotta and pink caught the light.

I moved close to a dirty double-glazed window then tried to peer in but all I could see were some diving cylinders lined up against the opposite wall. Wandering round the large bungalow there was a satellite television dish fixed up on a gable above the lean-to that housed a compressor for filling air tanks. Two small children stood mutely beside a rusty swing in the next garden, staring straight at me.

As I looked in the window I noticed a change in the air round me and realised that the drumming had stopped. I squinted out to sea: the figure stood up quickly on the raft, the dripping line nearest the drum set cleared the surface and the figure used it to pull himself in, towards shore. When he was closer he secured the drum-raft and got into a small, moored kayak which he began to paddle towards me.

'Hello,' I shouted.

The bow of the kayak scraped onto the shingle. I noticed, written in thick, silver marker all over the battered orange fibreglass, carefully lettered phrases . . . 'And the merchants of the earth will weep and lament' . . . was one I could decipher.

The man stepped out, sinking both his boots in the water

over their tops, but he didn't flinch, just stared at me; he was wearing a diver's jacket over a T-shirt that read: *I Hate Oasis*.

'I'm *loud*, man. I have to play out there or the neighbours' children can't sleep; I play the drums loud, man!'

'Right,' I nodded.

'Jazzrockfusion that's my bag, man, right? Mouzon or Cobham or Williams: who was the greatest; *that* is the question, my friend, that is what I use to judge a man. Who do you think was the greatest drummer?'

'Ah, I don't follow music much. Verve are good.'

'You a city man?'

'Mainland.'

'That's grave enough, my friend.' He sooked out of the water and bandied his way over to me still nodding.

'I understand you have some salvage I could be interested in: an aircraft propeller?'

'Salvage. *Salvage* is it? Some kind of collector are we? Is it sunken spoil that's your thing, gold *ducats*, silver *chargers*? Or are you the straightforward upright man who prefers to insert his unwashed penis into the mouths of children?'

I took a step backwards but he crunched past me and said, 'When our myths fade we must revitalise them. Understand?'

I shrugged.

'Re-vitalise,' he muttered, then giggled. Suddenly he spun and pointed to a complex of railings and planking moored off the rocky point. 'Brown crabs in my keep cages. Good money per crab but someone's robbing them and it ain't no seals; seals are my friends: if I play good and steady they jump up onto my raft. A seal can suck out a fish through the net

163

and an eagle will take a lamb in a land where death has no mercy. How did you get here?' he frowned.

I shrugged, 'I'm on my way to Ferry Slipway along the coast, I just wanted a peek at this prop out of curiosity.'

'Well you know what happened to that cat.'

'Did you find it about five hundred yards offshore about a mile south of the threshold out at The Drome?'

The Argonaut was walking away.

'Mr Scorgie,' I called.

He was walking towards the end of the pebble beach where a curve of rocks overlooked his keep cages.

Very dark, then the gentle swelling and dying of the lighthouse on top of the summer colony steeple. Sometimes I could see a pale line of surf tip and froth close in to the rocks.

I heard the slopping of the whisky as he thrust the bottle, from a Spar or Co-op, out of the darkness. I saw the pencil of light from the steeple canter across the sea towards us: it bloomed in our eyes then juddered off over the plateau of rocks to our rear. I swallowed some booze back and said, 'I'd love a cigar.'

'*A cigar*, is it?' Argonaut mumbled.

'These rocks are destroying my arse, I'm tired and I was wondering . . .'

'Look, look, do you see it — see that out there?'

'What?'

'Out there, 'bout sixty feet, 'bout fifteen fathoms — wait, wait till the light has passed.' The white beam from the lighthouse came spratting over keep cages, highlighting the hand-railings on the walkways. 'Do you see them too?'

I looked at the blackness then, made visible in the convex portions of the low swell, I saw lights, electric torch-lights below the water. 'I can see them, I can see them too,' I said in a hushed way. They were moving very slowly towards the keep cages.

'You see them, eh?' The Argonaut laughed and stood up.

'What are they?'

'Divers: the holiday cottage around the point there. They've cut the wires at the bottom of the cages. Here.'

He passed me a little bong that he must've had hidden at the spot. The dope smoke went down me clean and creamy and perfectly cooled. The Argonaut took his blast then he screwed off the top and drank out the coolant water from inside. 'A mix of brandy and water,' he explained. The Argonaut stood up and announced, 'Come on and I'll take you for a pint; you'll get a cigar in the pub.'

I jumped to my feet and followed him down the rocks in the darkness, beneath the stars which were wobbling above us unsteadily.

I said, 'I didn't think there was a pub on this side of the island,' following the Argonaut's deviating route down a steep track, bare rock skittering under my boots. Then I heard the shallow clucking of waters and the Argonaut commanded: 'Get in here.' He seemed to be kneeling down then I realised he was sitting in a small outboard boat tied to the rocks. 'Eh, right.' I stepped over the gunwhale and put my arse down as the outboard's engine splattered into life and immediately throttled up; the boat leapt forward, jumping over the black water: my shoulders hit the planking and for a mute instant I saw my erect leg point straight up and my steel-toed boot saluted the thin sliver of moon.

'Jesus *Christ*. Can you see where you're going?' I shouted up at the night sky.

The Argonaut's voice came out the darkness: 'You just lie and enjoy the voyage,' and being stoned off my cock that's what I did. My cheek against the inner membrane of the boat, I saw the stars slowly wheel round the sky above me, and felt the quick trembling of the water below.

When I sat up we were moving round in a wide, tracing arc, leaving a curve of moonlit froth behind us. There was a clustering of lights on the shore. This was a part of the island, despite my vow to explore every inch of it when I landed, which I had never seen.

The Argonaut closed down the power and the bow of the boat gracefully fell down. I saw a single fishing vessel tied up at the pier. Our boat slipped past and manoeuvred in to the side of the pier where there was a small stone slipway. He tied up and we stepped onto dry land.

At the top of the slipway I looked over towards a building, gold-coloured spotlights pointed up to a sign which read:

THE OUTER RIM HOTEL & BAR

Outside, with two guys leaning against it, their elbows up on the roof, was a parked, silver Opel Manta ennobled with chrome wheel-fittings, tall aerials and fog-lights. Six or seven fat candles were placed on the car's roof – the flame light made the vulgar car look strangely beautiful, as if it was about to be used in some religious procession.

The Argonaut sighed, 'Ah, the whelk-pickers must be abroad. Here come some of them now.'

I turned; I could see a set of car headlights crossing the dark waters towards our shoreline but there was no road or bridge way out there, only black water, yet there were the headlights moving across the surface of the sea.

The Argonaut explained, 'It's a DUCK amphibious vehicle that can go on land and sea; purloined from the army, no doubt.'

I saw the vessel's headlights approach the beach and it mounted up onto the land on wheels, great scooshes of water flooding off its flanks. I heard catcalls and yells and whoops. Myriad little points of light began to bob then fall from the rear of the amphibious vehicle: it was a large gang of young men with little lamps, like coalminers', attached to their nodding foreheads by little straps.

The Argonaut explained: 'Halogen bulbs. They're over for the Low Tide Festival. They'll get all *inspired* up in the Outer Rim Bar there; a few tokes then at closing time out on the shore and pick whelks until the tide comes up at dawn – they collect a few ton of them – late tonight you'll hear their voices, calling to each other in the dark; they're quite the crew: so wasted they all think they're extras in Star Trek. You know, they breed up children just to be whelkers?'

We walked towards the two men standing by the car with the candles on top of it.

'Ahoy, it's the Argonaut come to grace our shores,' shouted one of the men who was wearing an illuminated halogen lamp on his forehead. When he addressed any words to me, I had to squint at him as the lamp shone in my face.

'Halley's Comet, how'reydoin pal . . .' said the Argonaut.

'Ohnosobadnosobad,' beamed the one called Halley's Comet. 'It's hoaching busy with us lot in there. Here,' Halley's Comet passed a joint across the car roof, 'Taste a little starlight from the Central Belt.'

I shook my head so it was passed to the man next to him.

The Argonaut said, 'Hey, this is Halley, this is the Superchicken – we call him that on account of his mentalness, he's no very scared of anything.' The Super-chicken was holding a big whisky and he nodded at me. 'Our friend here's a Mainlander looked for some bitter salvage.'

Halley nodded gravely, 'He might get some.'

The Argonaut asked, 'Car out the night; what's up with the bikes?'

Superchicken replied, 'Well, I come in the living room this afternoon and the bastarding wee brother has the Yamaha, completely dismantled, spread out across the carpet on bits of newspaper.'

'Bit of a fucker if you're in a hurry,' Halley added.

Superchicken looked at him, paused a few seconds, then said, 'Just a bit of a fucker all together.'

'What about the Suzuki?' asked the Argonaut.

'Steering wobble. Tried to ride through it on the long straight road at the point. The steering wobble started about seventy-five mile an hour. Tried to accelerate beyond it but when I got to eighty miles an hour I was finding the handlebars really difficult to hold in position, tank-slapping like crazy. When I got to ninety-five miles an hour I was taking up both lanes of the road going from side to side.'

'Jesus, that's a serious wobble, man,' nodded Halley, his forehead lamp flicking up and down the car roof.

The Superchicken said, 'Aye, mind you, the steering wobble disappeared at a hundred-and-twenty-five.' Superchicken shrugged grimly then swigged from the whisky.

The three men talked on like this for a time. At one point the Argonaut mentioned a body he'd taken from the bottom of the sea, a whelk-picker who had fallen from the amphibious vehicle one year: the last thing they had seen was his yellow-coloured forehead lamp shining below the surface of the night-water then fading like a candle as it sunk away down, the pale white hand still outstretched.

I must've been still stoned listening to their ravings. I was looking up at the sign on the building.

'Outer Rim of what?' I suddenly asked.

Halley looked at me, 'Outer Rim of *everything*,' he shrugged.

'Away in there and get your cigar and get us two drams, tiny triples, ice in one, eh?' The Argonaut held out a twenty-pound note which I almost snatched.

As I stepped inside The Outer Rim Bar, virtually everyone was wearing an illuminated halogen lamp on their heads – the individual beams cutting through the smoky dark air of the place. I pushed my way to the front.

Leaning on the bar I noticed a girl who had no lamp on her head; however she did have an electric kettle instead of a handbag. I could see her make-up things and stuff inside it. As I scrutinised a bit closer I noticed she had a stocking, all balled-up and hanging out of the bottom of one of the legs of her jeans.

To my dismay the barman had on a halogen lamp as well. I looked up at the whiskies and said, 'Eh, two Whyte & Mackays; triples please.'

'Do you want ice in either of the whiskies?'

'Ice in the Whyte but not in the Mackays, please!'

The barman glared at me, his lamp shining right in my face.

'Ahm, just ice in the one please.' I looked at the selection of cigars which was nothing special. 'Can I have a Hamlet as well, please.'

The barman said, 'Plain, cheese, Spanish or mushroom?'

'Pardon?'

'Plain, cheese, Spanish or mushroom?'

'What, the cigar?' I said to him.

The barman said, 'Cigar? Oh! Hamlet! I thought you asked for an omelette. It's your fucking accent.' He shook his head, plucked a cigar from the tin and dropped it on the bar with my change.

The girl with the kettle was looking in my direction. I smiled and, nodding to the crowded room full of drunken people with lit-up foreheads, I yelled, 'We'll be okay if there's a fucking powercut.'

The girl just stared at me.

'Here for the Low Tide Festival?' I asked.

'I'm here to try and get laid; I don't have any friends but I've got a packet of Mates in my kettle.'

'That's the most beautiful chat-up line I've ever heard,' I said.

'Who says it was a chat-up line, you fucking wank!' As she

walked away I noticed a pair of lime-green knickers emerging from the bottom of her other trouser leg.

Back outside I handed the Argonaut and Superchicken their whisky. Halley had rolled another joint. I lit my cigar by leaning over to a candle. I could feel the men had been talking about me when I was inside the bar.

Suddenly Superchicken explained, 'We're in the habit of using candles cause we keep running the batteries flat by having the headlights on out here.'

'Very pretty,' I smiled weakly, watching a candle flicker under the little glass that sheltered the flame.

The Superchicken said, 'Look the crack's going to be crap here with whelk-picking going on; I'm taking a drive over to Sweetbay, come along, we could light a driftwood fire on the sands.'

'Nah, I'm staying put. Business here,' said the Argonaut.

Superchicken started puffing out then chipping the candles from the roof of his car and tossing them in at the passenger foot space. 'I'm just going over for an hour or two; no into it?'

'Nah, can't be bothered,' shrugged Halley.

Superchicken stooped and climbed into the car, we all stepped back as it started up.

I said, 'Sweetbay, that's an amazing sounding place.'

'That's the original Gaelic name for it,' said the Argonaut, 'Sweetbay. Centuries ago some old greyhead had second sight that one morning all these little children would walk down the sand to the water's edge and drink the salt water which was sweet; then it was always called Sweetbay. But when I was a kid, in 1975, this barge *The Lusitanos*, got stuck out on the reed beds then sunk; it was carrying ninety tons of sugar that became invisible salvage: it all dissolved, and for a week all the kiddies could walk down on the sand, lift the seawater to their lips and it was sweet.'

We watched the Opel Manta move forward onto the pier then turn expertly, stopping just before the edge – the long nose of the car butting out once on the forwards suspension and the full beams pointing out to the dark sea. The pitch of the engine changed as it revved backwards fast, reverse lights illuminating the rising mast of the fishing boat behind. The headlights of the car shone directly at us and I held a sheltering hand to my eyebrows just in time to hear a thump, the back of the car jumped then, for an amazing instant, I saw the headlights rear into the air sending two spectacular beams upwards through the night sky . . . There was a loud impact and I saw the mast of the fishing boat tip itself slightly towards us.

'Oh, fucking *Jesus*, the Superchicken's finally gone over the edge of the pier,' shouted Halley. Already figures were running over the wooden pier to the edge of the structure.

When we got to the edge it was to find the Opel Manta at a forty-five degree angle, its rear rammed onto the middle of the fishing boat's deck. The front wheels were resting on the edge of the pier, the radiator just showing above the bollards' level. Superchicken was still sitting smugly at the steering wheel with his arms folded, reclined back on the angle: he had wound down his window. 'How about *that* for fucking double parking,' he barked, and suddenly switched on his hazard warning lights.

Argonaut shouted, 'Get out the car, you arse, those moorings might go and I'll be grinning at your puss on the bottom.'

More whelkers were piling from The Outer Rim Bar and looking down on the boat, their head-torches darting and circling on the planking of the deck.

In a slow continuation, Superchicken crawled into the back seat, opened the rear door and slid out, his belly showing as his Motörhead T-shirt pulled free of it; his running shoes dangled a moment then he stood on the deck of the boat.

Halley warned through clenched teeth, 'Skipper Murdo's no going to appreciate it when he sees the burroch.'

'When's he due to go out?' asked the Argonaut.

'Soon. With this tide I can't see him waiting for a crane (he pronounced it 'cranee') to come over from the garage on the other side of the island.'

'Not for a garish heap-of-shit-car like yon,' Argonaut nodded seriously.

A few of the whelkers helped the Superchicken up the ladder; when he got onto the pier they started clapping his back as if he'd achieved something.

'No bother, no bother,' Superchicken announced.

The Argonaut sent me to the bar with Superchicken to buy him a stiff one. While someone went in search of the First Mate on Skipper Murdo's boat, the whelkers began making their way down the shoreline for their night's strange harvest – they were shouting and stooping, a crazy swarm of tiny light bulbs, weaving, clustering and separating along the darkened beach.

It was soon established that the deck planking of the boat was intact, no damage done, so all Superchicken could do was watch as the First Mate arrived, looked at the canted vehicle, shook his head and said, 'This takes the biscuit, this does.'

They let go the forward mooring and the car crashed down on the deck as the boat swung outwards.

I stood on the pier. A squad of whelkers and the Argonaut held the car secure as the boat turned astern and sailed out into the weak dawn light, listing badly to port, before the men on deck hoisted the Opel Manta – with its aerials, spotlights, sports steering wheel and trimmings – then, in about a hundred feet of water a quarter of a mile out, threw the car over the side; it hesitated on the surface a moment then was sucked under in a twist and swirl of froth.

Everyone began to reconvene in The Outer Rim Bar.

I awoke to shouting and couldn't remember who or what I was. Something was stuck to my face. I sat up from the hard floor I was on. Pain seemed to be shuttling from left to right and back again in my head. I remembered: I'd crossed back to the Argonaut's house. He had the propellor hung on the wall of his long, empty living room, with the carpet that smelled of the sea, the wallpaper scratched and marked up to waist height, the roof tiles of the mad house all different because

Argonaut himself had raised them from two sunken barges, using buckets and winch.

After smoking another hookah-full, Halley and the Argonaut had shrugged on air tanks and masks, put the regulators in their mouths and, carrying the equipment, walked into the water to rig the keep cages with explosive charges.

I'd stayed, drinking, as their torch-light crawled under the surface of the bay. When I'd needed to crash out later Halley had pointed to the box room, 'There's a sleeping bag in there.'

I looked around me: up the walls, on the floor and in my hair the little polystyrene balls adhered with static. The sleeping bag was lying in a corner. There was no light or window in the room; in the darkness I'd ignored the sleeping bag and shoved my shoes into a beanbag, ripping open the lining and pulling the torn fabric up to my chin. I thought it was a bit tight when I'd squeezed in.

In front of the house Argonaut was shouting:

'You stoned-out bampot, that's lime cordial.'

Halley's Comet had fried all the bacon and egg in what he thought was olive oil from a bottle in the scullery.

Nam the Dam's Westland came lifting over the high ridge above us, circled the bay, blowing up spray, then landed somewhere along the shore.

It was twenty minutes before I recognised Brotherhood's walk coming along the beach.

I nodded to him.

'Afternoon everyone. I'm so pleased to find you; thought

you might have left the island, our little Forbidden Planet where we can play at The Tempest daily.' He nodded back to where the helicopter had landed in a field: its stopped rotors, long and drooping; sheep cautiously moving closer. 'My father is dying; have to send for some specialist equipment from the Mainland, could I have a private word?' He threw an arm round Argonaut and manoeuvred him southwards along the shore. When he returned he said to me, 'You left without saying bye.'

'It must've slipped my mind.'

He paused, waiting for me to ask about her, so I didn't. He knew how strong I'd been to walk away so suddenly, my absurdist repertoire exhausted. He knew my humanity was a defeat over him so he'd been searching the hills in the helicopter, perhaps hoping to find me next to the corpse of the skinned, emaciated kangaroo.

'You don't know, do you?'

I sighed.

Brotherhood said, 'I almost didn't realise. God knows, we've all been distracted with this millennial rave: El Big One. Promotion, busy pockets of the youth of today; look to the future, friend: mobile phones and jackets that say Security, don't you see that vision of the future? All is in the hands of the youth. All our hopes!' he laughed. 'God, man, don't you see the reason she stayed, little mummy tiger, the jumpers on all the time? Look, just a thought for you to take with you on your trip to the Mainland, so when you think back to your times here you can think of me, playing happy families . . .'

'Brotherhood, what are you on about?'

'I can imagine our wedding night,' he sighed and, genuinely pensive, looked out to the keep cages, 'She'll roll over away from me, curl up her legs, "You can just go rampant on me from behind," she'll announce, and that'll be our wedding night. Then I'll be able to howl with laughter at the little bastard thing driving its pedal car or whatever up and down the corridor and as the winter nights approach once again, I'm looking forward to the Old Pleasures that I gave up so long ago. If the hotel is shut it won't be one of the Brand New Wives, I guess it'll be a sixth-former from the boarding school – whatever, both her and the other girl's mouth playing Russian roulette with my cock . . .'

I punched Brotherhood on the jaw and it was a pleasure to hear his next words snap shut. He sat down heavily in the shingle then a blow, denoting side-taking had begun, sent my head snapping to one side and I hissed out snottery black blood onto the back of my hand.

I was sitting in the shingle too, facing Brotherhood, the Argonaut looming above me.

Brotherhood spoke and spat, then continued. 'You didn't know at all. I knew you weren't that strong. When you left, for a moment I thought you knew, so I was afraid, but you're just as stupid as me. She was pregnant the day she walked into the hotel.'

The Argonaut helped him up, took two steps towards me and kicked me on my ear, I fell to the side.

'You'll sleep better at nights, I'm sure. I had to say goodbye. You've been fun, by far the best I've ever known in fact. Enjoy civilisation.' He crunched back up the shore then turned, 'What is your real name?' When I just glared at him he added, 'We could have named it after you!' He walked off. The starting motor on the chopper whined and the Argonaut said, 'He told me about you. Fake compensation forms. I'll give you your propeller all right.'

In front of his bungalow, with the dumb children staring, the Argonaut stripped off my shirt. He lashed the propeller to my back so its weight was across my shoulders; a burning point of pain at the base of my spine started straight away.

'Four mile along the coast is Ferry Slipway, they'll untie you there.' The Argonaut looked at me and laughed. 'You're lacking your crown of thorns.' He walked away to the rocks and I began to stumble forwards. Argonaut soon caught up with me. He was cradling a large clear jellyfish with purple central tracings, he draped it ceremoniously over my hair so its cold blubber cooled my forehead.

'Your regalia: unfortunately not a stinger.'

'A reminder of your ancestors,' I forced a smile and began walking.

Moving through birches and whins further along the shore I had to turn first this way then that and move between trunks sideways. It was when I was clear of The New Projects on the lonely coastline, I turned, and with the propeller on my back, I shook free the jellyfish and began to climb back over the mountains in the direction of The Drome Hotel.

I was near the summit of the ridge when the keep cages exploded in a low plume of white water, shattered crabs rattling down out of the sky onto the coloured tiles on the roof of the Argonaut's house.

THE LETTER

Secret Address
Let's say Tierra del Fuego
(use a second-class stamp)

Dearest Pa-Pa (nearest I'll ever have),

Found this paper: so smooth to the touch, like the flat tummy of a twenty-year-old girl, eh? some time back in a hotel of no return, an island at the end of the world, there was a couple who had proposed marriage to each other live on national radio! I'm still unmarried, though I've had an interesting clutch of suitors lately. I'm writing to tell you I got up the clout and you're a grand-daddy if not a very grand person. Perhaps you've let your last breath hiss out your nostrils? Couldn't care less but I thought I'd try dement you one last time with the story of the events leading up to my child's birth and The Nativity itself.

The things I've seen in the last years! Listened closely to my body and done what it told me – obviously! – and mainly otherwise read books while drinking sweet coffee all over Europe.

Daddy, a man swam the Danube for me! Are you proud? It's full of minging ex-communist pollution. I'd just got off a very bumpy flight from Stockholm, or was it London? Whatever, rushed by taxi (the driver had a conversation with himself all the way) to a basement where the man had lived in a cage existing on spring water for forty days and nights; it was somewhere in the Romany district, the seventh or eighth precinct, then sparks flew in the candlelight from the saws they cut the bars with while a man played a didgeridoo. The air was mouldy and it was full of journalists' whispers – there was a crew from CNN and concept artists galore, studying the shadows.

The man made a huge speech on his experience in a language I understood nothing of. He ate a chunk of bread and sipped a thimble of wine that comes in nine levels of sweetness!

By sundown the fool was doing the crawl through muddy water – right across and almost back to our metallic café table when the River Police got him: shame. I folded his trousers neatly on the chair-back opposite and left enough money for the bill. He wasn't the Jesus I'd crossed Europe for; I found him later, in the hotel, but more of that when I feel like it. I ensconced myself in The New York Café: beautiful, handsome rude waiters in white jackets (slept with two); a piano player; brilliant pastries, all crazily priced. I asked the old piano player who specialised in Strauss to play Where It's At by Beck, and fucked if the old one didn't launch into it! We became friends but never lovers though I stripped for him once. Christ, he must've been eighty and I learned things. I used to enjoy making the two young waiters jealous of him!

But listen, Daddy, this is not all! I had a conversation about post-modernism! It's true. I actually said the ridiculous word and even held my sandwiches with two fingers. That was at a university. (Going back to The New York Café: its walls were impregnated with the evil and torture and executions of the old regime who used to own it, impregnated the same way they were, browny-yellowed by the slowly rising Havana smoke.)

I've *so* many stories I could tell you – infuriating itch – I hope every one of my words will be like the bedsores which bloom on your bony arse as you die – unable to scratch your knuckles up into the jelly.

I've only wrote 3 letters ever before. I can remember word for word I think: one was to Orla, my girlfriend in Sweden:

Sture Hof Tues

Orla, I'm on my sixth Bloody Mary, you know they always mixed a cracker here.

Look, there's other men besides him – and ones who sweat less from their armpits, though few with so cute a frown: I know you believe he should give up his gold-leaf paintings that light the single room at dawn . . .

Ooops . . . you guessed it – as I walked in bare feet over his latest canvas entitled: *Psychedelicatessen* (stretched out on the floor with piles of the Swedish translation of my novel holding down each corner) I trailed silver and gold prints into the bathroom.

. . . I know you think you should live by those damp lakes of your homeland, him being the mosquito-bitten house-husband while you bring the bacon home in your blue Saab, giving out enemas and bunion plasters with equal generosity; him waiting for you, shuffling the wok as you swing the car keys but *for fuck sake* girl, when did you start believing in all this bourgeois stuff? This is *not* the Orla of old.

I thought of your lovely eyes and the way you use the Rimmel liner, cause you *know* you'll be crying at some point every Saturday night. I'm deluded there's a scrap of innocence and humility still left in me – but I've taken my young heart and polished it perfectly smooth.

I really suggest you put down your Anatomy and we meet this evening at the Sture Hof eight p.m. for Bloody Mary and laughs. Forget him and his Mathieus and Kandinskys and others who look like they suffered from severe flash headaches; that's just you taking seriously the middle-class world we had agreed to rip off.

Orla, the fact is, his gold-flecked fingernail has been up my arsehole all last night and most of this morning: Yum yum!

Kisses on your opening which I've
spared yet again.

PS. A definition of human evil might be our ability to use those cutey-pie pet names we have for each other (Goolah-Goosh, Smicky-Smooch, Beeper) – whispering them to a complete stranger I'm fucking. I used *every* one of our names on him last night. Some betrayal, eh?

I'll buy the drinks. Mmmm and kisses.

Like that one? I'll transcribe another later, after I've fed the baby. Autolactation, it's a scream, Father.

I'm not going to tell you where I'm hiding out. You're too dumb ever to find me; besides, I hear you've developed agoraphobia and can't leave the village limits! Hysterical. The place I am has lots of stones. All its monuments are stone too. There's a big stone up the mountain round the back. Local myth has it, if you can put your arms round and touch fingies you can make a wish! I got my long monkey arms round it . . . obviously the wishing front is pretty bleak for pregnant women! Christ, I could barely see my toes at the end but the weight just fell off after I dropped the egg. I've been cycling up to the stone and making a wish each day. As I've got skinnier my rings chink thegether.

Becoming a fat cow fair gets you out a few niggling situations. I had a crappest job ever on yon island, house-maiding, kitchening, and a waitress. Housemaiding ended in wrapping all the mattresses in newspaper at the finish of season to keep damp out all winter long; the words 'pillowslip' and 'bolster' leave my nose curled and always will. What a pain in the cunt, beyond all belief, but better than the alternative: sleeping with creepy John Brotherhood the owner. You know how Robinson Crusoe thought that print in the sand came from Satan? Well it was more likely John's! I set down my terms: 'Just go rampant on me if you want but it'll be from the behind; my rear-end out, with me curled on my side and, though I doubt it, if there's anything down there in the piston department you'll be going real easy else the tip punctures me inside and the foetus comes spilling all out and Hotel Linen Service'll be loving you again for the most messed in the west AND talking of which, you'll be wearing not just one condom but *two* Superstrongs, one over the other so I doubt you'd feel much even if you were balling the mincer in the kitchen; I might have messed up in the contraceptive department in the past, but I'm fucked if I'm getting the virus offof a Tory.'

His face soon turned sour at all that: typical squeamish misogynist, it's always fears about hygiene at the bottom of yous, fear of the body, cause you've never known how to give pleasure or enjoy it.

I best start some of the stories culminating in the birth of my baby.

You know how Satan has all the best music? well the Devil's Advocate has got every one of his albums. You could start like this:

The Devil's Advocate opened his eyes, whites vivid in darkness as he rose up from his lair knowing the time of my confinement had come to an end; his fat legs had been splayed apart where he was laying, meditating along the length of the stunted, horizontal larch. His face smeared in mud, he began to walk down into the enclosures and out-houses – moved through the shaking portable generators, the cables lying still like oil-runs, the fairground vehicles on the airfield site. Wandering peacocks scuffle aside to let the Devil's Advocate pass, the lasers flicking left and right in the night are flecking on the screens of fanned feathers: the central tail-vane white in moonlight. He slaps the rumps of the circling ponies, the drugged-out kids gingerly holding the reins in their thin fingers; but this was all later when Lucky People Center were speeding it up in the big tent. I was up the stairs in The Heated Rooms where old Brotherhood had died. I was lying still stunned, obsessed you could say, by the modern pilgrimage of the one who pretended to be the Aircrash Investigator: haunted by the day I saw his Christ figure appear on the skyline, arms outstretched like some Icarus as he jogged down the slopes of 96-Metre Hill, past the stunted larch, the trousers torn where he had stepped over the barbed wires, his face beaten by the ones over at The New Projects.

I have the skill of noticing things; that much you can make a song and dance about: like on a rainy day in the city when you have enough for a taxi you wonder why the wetness on the vehicle floor is only on the left-hand side, till it dawns on you: that's the pavement side where almost all are going to be getting in through.

Before the millennial rave, it was me first noticed the far-distant helicopter with the black speck hung below it like as its own vertical sunlight shadow, bumping over the surface of the Sound. Closer it came till clear: the astonishment that it was a big bed dangled on the rope and spinning slowly beneath the helicopter, above the tips of the pine plantation that fashed shyly, left and right in the downdraughts.

This was the bed of sand for Brotherhood's dying father. The special strengthening support struts, sledgehammered into place, were so close together in room 7, below Brotherhood's Heated Rooms, that yous had to turn sideyway to get from one side of the room to the other and pocket some of the soft toilet paper as relief from the agony-stuff Brotherhood had lumbered us with out in the caravans.

Brotherhood's father was laid out then on the bed of sand. Opportunistic viruses, papa: lovely. Then the one in his spine started heralding the arrival of the Frame. The upper section of his spine was turning to a jelly; to continue eating the milky porridge I brought up to him – my big belly that he wanted to touch, jutting out – and so's could sit upright to eat, the Frame would be bolted onto him: a structure of metal rods clamped to his collar-bones and secured round his forehead, his lips slowly moving like a tortoise, through the space where I passed the spoon, between the bars – the structure preventing his head crushing his neck in a final shrug. His skeleton was sinking down through the ocean of his organs as the oxtail soup of bad piss gathered in the catheter bag; then his tears, not the sadness of this end but the humiliation of the big spot on his nose – his wasted body still having the strength to produce *that*. Acquired Immune Deficiency Syndrome, Dad; that's what Brotherhood's father died of. Had off the French lassies who dived from the wings of the seaplane and swam, bobbing towards him, the summer water glistening on their foreheads.

But what was most on my mind was the Odyssey, the crossing made by the man with the propeller. When he had appeared on that lantern skyline and stumbled back into our domain I turned away from the window and raced down the spiral stairs (with one hand on the banisters); I ran up the drive, the canvas shoes sinking into the brown, clayey, puddly bits. I saw Brotherhood appear from the boathouse direction carrying the shotgun he'd been pigeon shooting with. Sudden I got the notion Brotherhood was going to shoot the man with his arms held out all helpless and racked up. As I walked towards him, Aircrash Investigator smiled and fell on his knees. I reached out and touched the cold metal of the propeller.

'It's the one. I came back. You're expecting.'

'Isn't that the truth,' I says and began untying the rope.

Brotherhood was laughing, standing on the other side of the barbed wire shaking his head. With both hands I let down one end of the propeller to the earth.

'Do what you want with him.' Brotherhood laughed.

I took him to the room full of the supports; then as winter deepened he moved from one freezing room to another at will, trying to find the warmest.

In my imagination I thought loads about his lone crossing – the propeller lashed across shoulders, under the changing skies from which dark winds came – those clear stars near the derelict tracking station – the hollow clangs of the abandoned observatory. Closely he passed, chin pushed into his chest – a flame, bright and warm as sirius-glint in the frozen air: a burning at the base of his long spine; always knowing if he stumbled forwards on his front he might never rise again. It became too dark to walk on, and he leaned backwards, rested the weight of the prop from Alpha Whisky upon the slanted generator roof of the telly-aerial bothy: stock-still all night, till the grey air was vibrating enough for him to move into the gold of dawn, his vision still troubled by animals patrolling near him in the darkness that had gone before.

Unable to drink for fear of man's ability to drown using inches of water, but singing out loud as he thought of the child unfolding week by week in my once-flat belly. Singing! So sheep jerked their heads towards him and unseen deer herds, that once belonged to the giants, flicked away uphill over the ridge as his tuneless voice cracked on. He crashed through the birch saplings bawling, Blue Ridge Mountains of Virginia, Lemon Tree segueing into Yellow Bird, Yellow Submarine, Flower of Scotland, the Corries' Glencoe, Nature Boy, Away in a Manger. Bark peeled from the winter trees, moles burrowed deeper for more convinced hibernation – the dead bracken-beds, crimson and burnished copper, broken stocks stomped lower, were lucky: spores deep buried for next year. On he came, careering through the singing woods, across the hollow of the dark grazings and down back braes, high on the plateau known as 'The Planet'; in dusk once more above the sole bulb of Boat Chandlers at Ferry Slipway, within earshot of the frightening shrieks of the military zoo, the childish chattering exhaust of the miniature train below, circling loudly over the switch points, the elder Grainger boy gripping the engine between his thighs, spitting into the metallic carbon-dioxide rush, 'The family will rise again, the aviary will burn; I'll be the hero, releasing the peacocks which that degenerate, Cormorant, wants to hire for this New Year ballyhoo at Drome – National Service for *the lot*; the days when the railways were great, each engine agleam; I will save the peacocks, releasing them to rut and breed throughout the grounds – their feathers erect like regimental colours, they'll mount, mount . . .' as he clicks the track using the remote facility fixed above the regulator, the train moves off up the papier-mâché tunnel to bring him, in his boiler-suit, to the dinner table, prompt . . .

Upward the skyline figure goes, this time racking the weight of the propeller on the lower branches of a larch and hanging there, till the pickings of some bird in his tousled head at dawn's first moan bring him onward: unhinging the prop and letting him become pushed down the sheep paths, feet pattering quick below the ridges – the telly aerial and the haze of disused masts from the tracking station, their different heights and rusted dishes sort of vertiginous monuments to the variety of private investors involved in the doomed station – whispers and frames of obscure aerials vivid in the morning sky.

On, to the end of the glen, the black cattle-drove roads flooded so he, for the first time, in the water around his feet, saw the image, the shocking ancient image he showed the world, reflected amongst the clouds in the clear, shallow floodwaters. Beyond he came to the dripping cliff, water rattering down the moss clumps so's he held his open mouth to the drips and his naked torso contracted and tightened as the icy water spattered it, yet it was here he leaned against the base of the wall, shivering till he slept. And dreamt his river-dreams:

Dark water took him as he stepped forwards – the weight

on his shoulders forcing him face-down and downwards, legs kicking, sinking, till his wide-open eyes reached the silt of the bottom, where he drowned – his body bloating up over the days, till its bags of swole air gently lifted the prop and all floated downriver, through the interior and out, into the sandy whorls of the delta, the ballooned Investigator turned with the propeller out into the bay where they swirled down among the burning phosphorus beds and twisting barnacled metal of Alpha Whisky. The distended corpse hanging, turning round slow in the sanded water, held up the propeller till the pincers of lobsters, caught in a force ten's up-swirl and briefly tangled in the body's mesh, snapped at the huge sac of rot-gas. Freeing a massive silver bubble and its satellites, which rolled surfacewards, the emptied corpse dove to the seabed till it became bones. A bubble of methane hoisted the skull surfacewards where a bobbing gull pecked out the remaining eye jelly, the heavy dunt driving the skull spinning down again, where it fell among the bubbling phosphorus bombs. Filling with their gas, the skull leapt to the surface once more, only to be cracked in two by the slicing prow of the *Psalm 23*.

All this he dreamed, before he picked his way through the night to the river's bank, illuminated by the burning islands of branches and twigs, circling down the glen. By keeping a steady pace, these passing islands of fire led the crucified figure along the lands, then the blazing pyres on the rock outcrops, shoreward of the loggers' camp and its porta-kabins . . .

He was sighted by Joe the Coal, driving fast along the glen

floors, the coal shed from the nunnery stuck on the back of the hydraulic lift; the nuns in pursuit, waving from the windows of their Morris Minor, missed the latest new miracle.

The Aircrash Investigator moved down through the Devil's Advocate's encampment; the Advocate himself, soup spoon frozen under his new goatee, watched the Aircraft Investigator stumble through his stream, swerve down to the first barbed-wire fence and step over it.

'She's pregnant,' he shouted.

'I know,' the Advocate nodded quietly, too softly for the Aircrash Investigator to hear. The wire squeaked as the Aircrash Investigator descended on to the wood-smoke of Drome Hotel, the Observation Lounge centred on the cross his body formed. Still with me, Dad? You should pay attention; you might learn something, extend your horizons, a wee bit edification: here's another letter.

Drome Hotel, Tuesday

Dear Mr Grainger,

You don't know me, and I only know you through a chance acquaintance and by dint of your social position on this island. What's important is I have no money, I'm pregnant and at the mercy of two or three particularly devious males. Back in April I pulled your daughter, who you really should teach to swim, out of the Sound from a wash-spilled launch, off Ferry Slipway. I put her on your Kongo Express home.

Now my thoughts have turned to my own child's

195

welfare so I'm asking you for £5000 to help me off this island and also for the use of your launch *The Maenad* that is currently assisting the construction of the tidal seal-pool at your zoo.

I'm a prisoner here so please visit soon. Don't bring any money. It's a nest of vipers.

Yours,
The pregnant housemaid.

No reply from that one, Pa. That's the aristocracy for you. Old Mr Brotherhood similarly lamented before he died, quoting O'Sullivan at Culloden, 'Oh, Sire, all is going to pot,' and what Walker Percy in *The Moviegoer* called 'the going under of the evening lands'.

Old Brotherhood had says, 'Listen, Lassie, come close so I don't have to shout. Tidy up your act for Christ' sake. You're pregnant, what's the short skirt for? Hard-ons have got both of us into enough trouble.'

We laughed, his lips slipping over his gums like a foreskin. He grabbed my hand. 'You've been good to me. Don't pretend it's easy for me. The doc is in every day now; bastard's usually asking about your belly. Just waiting for the hour he can really crank on my Diamorphine,' And, Papa . . . this is truly what he says, 'Come close, love. Now listen. After I'm gone you must promise me to do something . . .' and I lean close and he whispers what it is he wants me to do. When he died he gasped 'It's just like Christmas!' The Devil's Advocate stood out on the open slopes of 96-Metre Hill, watching Brotherhood Senior's burial with binocs.

There was just me, the Aircrash Investigator, Chef Macbeth, Brotherhood, the man from the council who worked the mechanical grave digger and the doctor who kept glancing at my belly.

Four took the cords and lowered the coffin into the hole. There was an awkward silence requiring a few words. Brotherhood shrugged, says, 'I told him way back they were tarts.'

I grimaced at the cold wind.

The men drank the Linkwood whisky. In the wind gusts that shook the closed hotel you could hear the sounds of the mechanical digger, jerking around in the cemetery. I was coming up the spiral staircase from the toilet. Brotherhood was on the way down. Here's what I told him, Dad. I put my hand on his shoulder. He smiled. The doctor laughed at something said by the Aircrash Investigator upstairs.

'My fostermother is buried in the graveyard. When she died a few greedy relatives turned up at the funeral; my fosterdad, in those days he still had a few guts left, he was still a good communist . . .'

'Hah,' Brotherhood knee-jerked.

'There was a lot of cash. Lots of jewels. Some that meant things to me. I would do anything to get those jewels back. And I need the cash. I would admire the man who could get those things . . .'

'Where are they?'

'To spite those relatives, to show he loved her, to show the root of all evil was below him, my fosterdaddy took those jewels, those handfuls of money, and he shoved them in the coffin with the corpse of the woman he loved before the undertaker bolted the top on . . .'

'Wow,' Brotherhood's eyes widened.

'. . . The stuff is still out there.'

'You're amazing.' He stared at me. 'What's the name on the gravestone?'

I told him. He looked at me a way I'd never seen him look.

He walked up the stairs, glancing back at me. Now Dad, don't go rushing over there till you've heard the whole story. I suppose these pages are shaking by now. Listen to me tell you about Christmas Day instead.

It was raining. There were still some leaves moving diagonally down from the stripped deciduous trees to plaster themselves on the wet grave slabs and against the roofless chapel, elevated up on its stairs so cattle couldn't graze inside.

Brotherhood had begun the day shouting 'Football in No Man's Land.'

He couldn't find a football, so a frozen turnip dug from the whitened earth of Gibbon's field had to do.

Up the hill went the men, towards the Devil's Advocate's encampment with its shorn tendril of tinsel hung on the nearby stunted larch – Chef Macbeth trailing, DJ Cormorant pointing upwards, gesticulating in the lead with his mobile phone held aloft like the staff of Moses, voices babbling from it, ignored. Brotherhood followed, tossing the turnip in his palms, trying to thaw it out; even the Aircrash Investigator had been persuaded from the boathouse where he spent all his time with my present to him, listening to the Andante

Con Moto once a day (allowing the failing batteries to revive).

'Out your trenches, you Bosche,' Brotherhood yelled.

The Devil's Advocate was wearing a long, enormous, sheepskin coat: sleet and hail adhered to the collar as he opened his arms in salutation through the flames of the big bonfire he built from the larches, felled in the dark, all save the solitary stunted, decorated one.

The game began: Brotherhood and the Devil's Advocate versus DJ Cormorant, Chef Macbeth and the Investigator. From the Observation Lounge, through the sleet, I could see their kicks raise plates of water from the ground. The game was called off when the Devil's Advocate tried to save with a header and was konked out. They tossed the neep into the flames and headed down, gathering wood on the way for the log fire.

Macbeth did oven-baked potatoes, another bottle of Linkwood had its top twisted off. We started playing pontoon around the fire in the Observation Lounge.

'Bust,' Macbeth slapped his hand down.

'I'm that sort, when passing a photocopying office in the city, I see *lamentation service* rather than *laminating service*,' says the Devil's Advocate and laid down a king of spades and ace of hearts. He touched the bump on his head.

'Ohh, bloody hustler,' Brotherhood moaned.

I told about the taxi floors. How I noticed useless things in cities.

When we were done playing pontoon the Aircrash Investigator invited everyone to the latest room where he'd wheeled the telly and video. Cormorant didn't come, he went on the airfield to supervise the arrival of the first generators, flown in by Nam the Dam.

We heard the chopper raising clouds of vapour out of the wet grass as we sat in 12, the men passing the whisky round. Aircrash Investigator started the video tape.

The scene began on the deck of *The Maenad*, Grainger in a kilt and the little one-eyed child smiling at the camera. Then the viewpoint swung around to show what at first looked like a long black snake following the boat in its wake, but you soon saw it was several seals dipping in and out of the froth, flanked by two dolphins. The scene cut to the jetty and there I was, tummy all enormous, smiling at Grainger and the wee brat. I could see her prim jaw move and could remember the words: 'It was her who saved me but she's not nice.'

Then the scene cut to a shoreline shot of *The Maenad* at anchor, the bob-heads of seals, dolphins and two divers around its red-and-white hull. The two derrick cranes reached out over the waters and two hammock-like bags hung down into the waves.

Next shot showed something disturbing the surface, then I watched the Aircrash Investigator's face as the erect, dynamic lines of the Cessna tailplane broke out and, slowly, the entire fuselage of Alpha Whisky hoisted up, gushes of brown water pouring from the ill-fitting doors and *The Maenad* was bowing in shorewards and bearing the slung wreckage of the now-risen sunken aircraft to the jetty. The next shots had shifted to the interior of the boathouse. A naked single bulb illuminated the wreckage of the two aircraft: united, like two fossilised dinosaurs, displayed across the deep black bottle-ends of the floor. A long, golden worm crawled from the barnacled wreckage and the Aircrash Investigator's heel crushed it against the upturned champagne bottles.

Finally we saw the Aircrash Investigator take the camera and turn it on the operator, it was the Grainger boy dressed in a British Rail uniform. He saluted seriously. The film fizzed out.

The Aircrash Investigator ejected the tape and started explaining what I'd heard, a good few times, before:

'Once I'd got the propeller off my fucking back, I was able to examine it closely. If you look at the end of it there's a tiny impact point with paint-traces. Those paint-traces match Hotel Charlie but the amazing thing was: they came from the lower rear fuselage.'

'So?' Brotherhood shrugged.

'It means: though he took off *first* he was *behind* Hotel Charlie. I'd been looking at it the wrong way round. When they both took off, somehow – and it would've been easy in the darkness – both pilots thought each was completely elsewhere: Hotel Charlie thought Alpha Whisky was ahead of him, Alpha Whisky thought Hotel Charlie was behind.'

'One overtook the other in their turn. Alpha Whisky came out of the final curve, probably checking behind him, pulled up and flew right into Hotel Charlie's blind spot. Once they touched both probably over-compensated to try and avoid collision. In darkness they both could have stalled or lost control. Whatever, the prop gashes tell me the whole story.'

'So, your work is finished.' Brotherhood smiled.

'I've still my report to complete,' the Investigator nodded to the Fisher-Price multi-coloured typewriter from the old crêche. Everyone laughed at the scattered manuscript, messily typed on the back of old menus and honeymooner's receipts.

Since it was Christmas, I did a few cigarette tricks, not inhaling, scooshing lighter-gas into pint glasses and burning it till we'd a nice blue cast to the room. I even filled the cellophane cig wrapper with smoke from a Silk Cut!

After Christmas, fires began to burn down on the airfield as Hogmanay approached. Macbeth would tie a firework to his remote-control aircraft and circle it through the night, ducking it in and out of bonfire flames. Tribesters arrived in tents, stalls, caravans, portakabins – *The Charon* came back into use, ferrying over from the Mainland while Nam the Dam's chopper delivered the heavy gear.

I kept close to the hotel, planning the end, understanding the time was near but hating the horribleness of not knowing when; the thing in my guts – the most spectacular tumour of all that I already loved – when would it come forth? The Devil's Advocate, still on the hill watching all, awaiting his time to come back down among us again.

Brotherhood had made several trips to the graveyard, under cover of placing imitation flowers, snipped from the fake dining-room tree, on his father's grave. He'd also taken to leaving apples and bananas that were rapidly nicked by the wee tribester girls, with their dreadlocks and doggies, camped down by the boathouse.

The Big One, DJ Cormorant's millennial dance party, was

to start on the night of the thirtieth and rave on till the new century came in at 31st's midnight. Cormorant had brought in all the right DJs, with Lucky People Center bringing on the moment over in the old tent they'd stolen offof one of the test platforms, drilling a few miles out into the seas. The entire tent had been silver sprayed with quotations from the bible – the nicking of the huge tarpaulin and the spraying was rumoured to be the work of the salvager, Scorgie Drumvargie, brother to the doctor on Mainland and often going under the name Argonaut. It was him had beaten up the Aircrash Investigator and almost killed him tying the propeller to his back.

Joe the Coal delivered the peacocks in his Bedford truck, shooing them out: purple feathers and faces besmeared with coal dust. It was also Joe who handed me the envelope with:

pregnant housemaid
Drome Hotel

and a big thumb's print in coal dust on the front. What a hoot, Dad; even you'll appreciate this. After rescuing the sunk aeroplane same way I'd rescued his half-blind daughter from the watery place, things had been playing on old Grainger's conscience; he'd come to the conclusion Aircrash Investigator had got me up the spout! His letter invited us to go work for him at the military zoo and seal pond 'as keeper to whatever animals you prefer; we've some animals in here from jungles, thing is we're not quite sure *what* they are.' And Aircrash Investigator was invited over as driver of the miniature train! We really got the hysterics imagining that perverse little domestic scene. The money was waiting for me at the castle.

Brotherhood complained about the noise all night at the start of the 30th. So I thought, the hell, and stole his cashmere overcoat from reception, stowed a little something in it, then headed out to the rave. Everyone was going totally bonkers. Saw one guy so out of it he was just standing still, taking his shiny jacket off and putting it back on again – he was actually getting quite a speed up and under those lights it looked really cool.

Bonfires were flaring inbetween the rave tents – empty bottles of mineral water kept banging and exploding as you passed, leaping out the flames. Peacocks stumbled around and folk were plucking their feathers – you kept seeing them in girls' hair.

It was near dawn when I met them, each with big joints all a-stumbly holding each other up and no girls near them.

'Telly-aerial repairers!' I shouted.

'Hey, hey it's the lassie from the boat at Easter there,' Redhead one says.

'You shower here *again*!'

'Aww, couldny miss this,' goes The Tall.

I went, 'So the tellies are out?'

'They've been out since Boxing Day.'

'Och, shame, all the poor grannies with no telly to see in Hogmanay.'

'Nah, nah,' went the quiet one, 'we're gonna sort that, promise, and DJ Cormorant's got us something else to do.'

'Aye. You just watch the hills up there at midnight. Here, by Christ you've been busy!'

'Who's the *lucky* man?' Redhead tried to grab me so I stepped aside and, despite, felt myself go beetroot.

'When're you due?'

'Bout week back.'

'Man, if these beats don't sook it out . . .'

'Right, okey-dokey, be seeing yous,' I went.

'Aye.'

'Don't be sailing now.'

'Haw, God bless you, lass, and all who've slept with you.'

I walked on, dusk seemed to be descending already. I saw a coloured fizzle in the sky and over by the slowly circling pony rides I saw Macbeth squinting into night air, holding his remote box.

At first I couldn't believe it, folk circling round, then I saw their plastic forks, their paper plates. The huge shire horse in the middle of them.

'Charlie?' I squints. Then I see the forester and as I walk up I'm even more astounded.

'Aye-aye, young lady, the nights are fair drawing in and especially for you I think,' says the brother, first-spoken as always.

'Hello, you two,' I smiled, not feeling so good for ages.

'You made off without saying bye to us . . .' says most baldy brother.

'Or Father.'

I held out both hands and First Spoken took and smiled. It

was then I saw it, beside forestry worker: a coffin, towed behind the horse, and the coffin filled full of steaming, red-sauced spaghetti that forestry man was dishing out to the ravers and collecting money.

'Good little earner,' smiled First Spoken. 'After Dad went, we had the joiner at Far Places knock up a seven-footer in pine with a walnut veneer.'

'The boy from the forestry came up with the idea.'

'We've done all sorts, Round Table, Rotary . . .'

'Weddings, parties; we can fill it with anything.'

'After trekking the hills with Papa . . .'

'Where did you have him buried – eventually?' I goes.

'We met some cattledrovers who had their lead beast tow father right out for us, with my brother clung to the beast's neck. The mobile phone was going all the way till it started to sink, then he cut him free and the current carried him out to the giant whirlpool . . .'

'Mariners tell us things can be caught in the whirlpool for years then spun out . . .'

'We may not have seen the last of the old fellow yet . . .'

The forestry worker called my name and came striding towards me.

'I've got something of yours,' I says as he kissed me on my cheek. I felt in my pocket, removed the knife and handed it to him.

'Oh no! You keep it. My God . . .' he nodded at my lump. 'C'mon let's go to the fairground later . . . coconut shy,' he says.

'All right, I've things to do though.'

'Me too. Coffin-loads of Vongole to sell.'

'How's your wife?' I goes.

'Now there's another story. Come say hello to Charlie.'

I walked up and clapped the big horse's snozzle. It looked with one black eye.

I leaned to the forestry worker and says, 'Stay away from the hotel; meet me at the graveyard, midnight.'

Down by the shore, on the far side of the tent with John Kelly giving it his greatest, I met these two tribester lassies, utterly beautiful, looking about fourteen and wanting to touch my tummy. They took me in their tent and rubbed my belly-button a bit, sooking down lovely-smelling northern lights.

'Och, why not, wee baby is almost there,' I goes and took a big sook.

'I felt a punch,' says the pierced-lip one.

'Kick,' I smiled.

'Does that mean it's a boy?' giggled the other.

Pierced-lip put her ear down to my tummy that looked all a-shine in the candlelight and says, 'I talked to her and she's a girl.' She smiled, then went, 'I've had my contacts in for two days.'

'Got any trips?' I goes.

When they give us them I fired two down and the one with the tattoo says, 'You're fucking far-out.'

'Wait to you see *this*.' I goes, and took the Advocate's gun out of my pocket.

Down by the water it was still loud enough. People were

dancing as I saw the spray of water, the two horns moving forward in the black water, thrashing up spray, the High-Pheer-Eeon clinging to the horns, kicking aside to sink down to his waist level, walk ashore and pick up a discarded burger that he just ate. The new lead beast came ashore lazily and more cattle began to make landfall along by the jetty; the boat carrying the cattledrovers pummelled into the shore, beardy jamp into the shallows and instantly shot his crossbow up into the sky. Macbeth's aircraft, trailing and spluttering a firework, fell into the Sound waters, momentarily aglow from random seabed phosphorus burnings.

I watched the headlights cross the Sound waters; the girl one of the drovers filming the amphibious landing on what a male correspondent would call *the beach head* – the girl, dashing up and down, right enough, as if dodging gunfire as the DUCK amphibious vehicle came up the stones. Super-chicken was driving and called out. 'I bought it; perfect vehicle for me, ya can't sink it!'

Whelk-pickers began to drop from the sides of the craft, halogen lamps waving and probing everywhere as they danced, immediately, some up to thighs in the water.

I stooped. The rower's back was hung with drying trout, his wide-shouldered sweep guntering shore-forth. The row-boat bumped over the seaweed onto the stones. I saw the rope behind suddenly lose its tautness as whatever the rowboat was towing sailed on in the darkness. I peered over the ridge and saw the Knifegrinder, hung with smoked fish, step ashore then I heard the thuddering beat of the kit as into the bonfires' cage of light came the drum kit on a raft, each transparent tom-tom filled with seawater and a small morsel of burning phosphorus – there even seemed to be some unfortunate goldfish inside the water-filled drums. The Argonaut, shirtless, flourished a final drum-roll, then, as the raft hit the stern of the rowboat he stepped off the drum kit, held his arms up and powered himself ashore.

I turned and shuffled through the dancers back towards the hotel. Brotherhood had issued me with a key to the front door. I let myself in, the beats of the Big One faint. I did my work in the kitchen, knelt and says a wee prayer.

Aircrash Investigator wasn't in his room. I shouted 'Hoi, Houlihan, Warmer, Failed Screenwriter. I don't care what you're called, only what you *are*. Come on.'

I was having difficulty reading my watch. As I locked the front door of the hotel I looked up towards 96-Metre Hill, saw the solitary fire ablaze. Holding my arms out before me I walked towards the graveyard.

A bonfire was burning amongst the graves and Brotherhood stood beside it smoking a cigar as a harassed-looking Macbeth excavated a grave using the council digger. 'What in Christ's name are they up to?' hissed the forester's voice out to my side. I was about to answer when I think my waters burst – anyway, all hell went loose in my guts.

The forester was helping me back to the hotel which was on fire. 'Too bad, too bad, it'll have to be here,' I snapped, as he let me droop to the ground in the turning place.

'No way, no fucking way,' and he dragged me to the garage and kicked in the door with real spectacularness.

Next thing, Dad, I'm being lifted somewhere: it's the rear of a Volvo hatchback that's been filled with hay. Worst of all it's a M reg!

The garage doors were wide open. I noticed, in my confusion, cause the drugs I'd taken were really getting busy with me now, a New Age family seemed to be living in our old staff caravans, they were ushering kids out the door. I was sure Quiet Life by Japan was playing on a radio somewhere but I couldn't remember the lyrics.

Smoke was swirling around and buggered if this one wasn't pulling off my Levi's.

'Hey, it's like a shag on the beach. You only need to take one leg of your jeans off.' I laughed, then I felt this weirdy muscle stuff and I pushed to high heaven.

An oily slab of smoke purled and whipped past the garage doors. A massive sheet of flame whipped up into the sky and some beams collapsed in the long extension corridor, the lights flicked on insanely, responding to the inhuman movements.

A window exploded then the curtains in the dining room tore outwards and erupted. The fire burned along the roof towards the pine plantation and through my tears I saw a string of trees lift up in a rush of fire, windows burst out and the roof tiles curled above the kitchens where I'd turned on the deep-fat friers earlier: full power, wet tea-towels over.

Soon, all the way down, the blockade of pine plantation was alight and, as my child was born in a burst of blood and the forester whirled her free, the smeared face of an ancient prophet or seer came close to mine, smearing a mucousy blood across one of my tits, nipple erect in smoke-driven breeze while the inferno of trees fell, some of them across the airfield, some of them collapsing into the graveyard, swiping down the grievous angels, the prudent crosses covering the grave of Brotherhood's father, his dream of torching the hotel complete, and of Carlton's now-robbed grave and the bright red hair of the mummified horror Macbeth had dug up – the random grave I had told Brotherhood was Mum's – the grave that yielded nothing, and the fire covered Mum's untouched headstone.

The forester took the knife he'd lent me and popped the umbilical, handed the knife back to me.

Sure enough, Devil's Advocate on the hill above had jerked open his eyes and screamed as he rose from his lair, white eyes wide; departing, as he arrived, in a plume of flame. He ran, sucked by the beat down that hill Carlton had once ascended: down into the burning enclosures and outhouses he came to the garage.

I was lying in the back of the car, my daughter under my chin. The Argonaut stood, hands held high, shaking. I had the big revolver pointed vaguely at him as the Advocate stepped in, scowled at the Argonaut and says, 'Who fired the hotel? Brotherhood?'

'Me.'

'Where's Brotherhood?' goes the Advocate.

'He was digging up in the graves.'

'So that's where he . . .'

'He's gone,' went the Aircrash Investigator who stepped

in. 'He had it hidden in Carlton's grave, must've put it there ten years ago. Inside the rotted ribcage no doubt.'

The Argonaut spoke, 'Just like the old resurrection men: dig up the graves of the unknown sailors and visitors washed onto shores, get them sealed in a barrel of brine then sell them to the Glasgow medical schools.'

'You shut your mouth,' growled the Advocate.

'She's crazy, man, already let loose one bullet.'

'You best give me that back. I've let you keep it long enough. You're safe with this man here.' The Advocate took the gun out of my hand.

I says, 'The three wise kings.'

They laughed. The Argonaut says, 'It's true, I followed the light in the eastern sky, Nam the Dam hovering overhead.'

'I dunno what you're so chirpy about, Brotherhood's bolted in your rowboat towing your bong-bong drums behind.'

'What! Bastard. Well, I've paid respects to the Messiah. I'm off.' Argonaut bolted.

'He says I was already dead,' I goes, Drowned. I'm in netherworld; purgatory.'

'You shot at him,' smiled the Investigator.

The Devil's Advocate says, 'I really suggest, before the forces of the state arrive, we all leave. My patience hasn't paid off; meanwhile . . .' He stepped out into the flame-lit night.

The Aircrash Investigator kneeled by me in the old car; he says, 'Haven't you and I heard the chimes at midnight.'

'Happy New Year,' I says, then, 'That means you've really lived, eh?'

'Yes, to the full,' he went.

I goes, 'It's from My Own Private Idaho.'

'Nah, it's Shakespeare.'

'Aye?' I went.

'Have you lived?' he says.

'Aye,' I goes.

'Will we . . . go . . . together, you, me?'

'Together,' I says. 'Us?'

He went, 'Yes. For always, with her.'

I thought of Brotherhood. What had happened to him. He was darting and zig-zagging through the groups of young people. Some were still arriving, gawping silently at the huge burning of the hotel, spilling from the disco bus; a tractor had drawn in a horse box that opened and young girls thundered out.

Brotherhood was casting a black shadow in the flame of his burned hotel. Wrapped tight and held to his chest: the filthy towel holding the shard of metal or plastic. As he wondered if even the ghost had come to dance, the wrapping fell free and the thing he was carrying bumped ahead of him. It hit the ground and seemed to bounce once, then suddenly it went rigid like metal, but at first it had changed shape with the impact. Forgetting the towel, Brotherhood stooped, picked up the fragment, and stumbled down the embankment, the Devil's Advocate chasing him, but Brotherhood was into the first boat he found and power-rowing out. The Advocate had screamed, sat on the shore and only then noticed the uncoiling rope on the drum-raft, the Knifegrinder slumped unconscious on its stool.

But the Advocate had to choose. On or until another day. As the drum set moved out into the waters of the Sound, the Advocate limped through the dancers, back towards the frazzling beams of the collapsed Observation Lounge.

After carefully placing the wreckage part in the bottom and rowing into the black sheet of the Sound waters, probed by the Oyster Skerries beacon, Brotherhood was halfway across before he realised he was towing something. He cast it loose. Next afternoon, Knifegrinder was awoken by a passing trawler far out in the ocean.

Brotherhood never saw *Psalm 23* till he heard the clean sheath of its prow – the still-going beats of the new century covered the ship's approach.

He reached for the fragment then the boards flew under him and he was in water. John Brotherhood trod water. Like a lightning storm far below him, the seabed flickered, showing the stomachy depth of the Sound. He stared and shivered with loathing after the stern of the car ferry, at his burning hotel half a mile away; then he began to swim, not back to the island, but kicking out onwards to the uninhabited banks below the mountain range.

'For always?' I says.

The Aircrash Investigator went, 'Here's the deal: I'll always hold the hair out your face while you puke.'

'Aye. All right then,' I goes.

There you have it, Dad; all you need not to know surrounding the birth of the beautiful grand-daughter I'll make sure you never see. Forgive my elliptical style: I want you to die in the maximum possible confusion. Don't dare even think of me on your death-bed.

When the fire engines had arrived they knew it was a dead loss, so the firemen danced in the big top where Lucky People Center were fashing it up. The firemen's reflective jackets looked fantastic in the lights.

We were headed other way, the flight into Egypt. The Advocate and the forester put me and my daughter in the coffin pulled by Charlie the shire horse – a bit covered in Vongole sauce but I was spattered with blood anyways – and off we slid, up the driveway, rumping over potholes and much nicer up the flanks of 96-Metre Hill. Old Charlie tugged us, the Aircrash Investigator following, smiling at me and the wee thing under our mound of blankets. For the first since coming to that island I wanted sleep but Aircrasher was pointing and forester was shouting, the Advocate staring up. Up at the tracking station where the Observatory once scanned the heavens, the telly repairers had got flashing semaphores diving and dotting, up and down and up and down the enormous aerials – each mast lighting up in different rhythm: chaos of blinkings, dyings and flourishings like God's Christmas tree: the entire sky seemed to be doing press-ups. I could see the stars lurking beneath the pulsars of masts and when I looked back at the Aircrash Investigator, a fantastic column of flame and smoke was over his shoulder. I lit a Silk Cut, Extra Mild.

Goodbye.

Morvern Callar